# SOMETHING TO
## *Hope For*

## CROSSROADS SERIES BOOK 1
# T.S. ROBINSON

# Something to Hope For

## CROSSROADS SERIES BOOK 1

## T.S. ROBINSON

NIGHT OWL STORIES

For my girls, no matter what life puts in your path, never give up, never stop living, never lose hope.

"In three words I can sum up everything I've learned about life: it goes on." **— Robert Frost**

# Contents

# *Prologue*

# DATE NIGHT

*"It is a curious thing, the death of a loved one. We all know that our time in this world is limited, and that eventually all of us will end up underneath some sheet, never to wake up. And yet it is always a surprise when it happens to someone we know. It is like walking up the stairs to your bedroom in the dark, and thinking there is one more stair than there is. Your foot falls down, through the air, and there is a sickly moment of dark surprise as you try and readjust the way you thought of things."*

— Lemony Snicket, Horseradish

"**D**inner was excellent. Thanks for surprising me," Laura said. She reached over the center console and held her husband's hand.

Joe responded with a smile and kissed her hand. "When I couldn't remember the last time we went on a date, I decided it was time."

"I'm going to text the kids and let them know we're on our way home." Laura let go of Joe's hand and reached for her purse to get her phone.

Deemed the "Mary Poppins bag" by her kids, that purse seemed to have anything a person could need. Illustrating that point, she pulled out a bottle of Tums and passed two to her husband while she kept digging around with her other hand for her phone. He popped them into his mouth without taking his eyes off the road. There were many small moments like this that they had shared over the years; the routine made it special.

Finally finding her phone, Laura sent a text to the kids, then sat back and stared out the window at the lights of the oncoming traffic. She hated I-81, always had, even as a kid. Busy and crowded at the best of times with tractor trailers hauling goods up and down the east coast, college kids traveling to and from the many colleges that lived off the exits, campers from the constant stream of vacationers and nature lovers, and finally the local traffic, like Joe and Laura, trying to get from one small town to another, made the highway constantly clogged.

Normally, they wouldn't have taken 81 as their small family farm wasn't far from town, but Joe had to go down to Broadway to get a part for their tractor before dinner. At least, that had been the plan. When they arrived, they found out the guy had just sold the part to someone else. Joe's brother, Rob, told him about a guy in Mt. Jackson that may have one, so after dinner they got what they needed. The tractor had stopped working nearly a week ago and they've been searching all over for the part. Now they were finally on their way home.

Laura's phone chimed with a new text. She grabbed her big bag and hauled it onto her lap to dig out her phone again.

"Benny says they're watching movies and eating pizza," she said, reading the text to Joe. "Tess is hiding behind a pillow. They're watching The Shining."

Joe sighed. "Are we going to have Tess sleeping between us tonight?"

"She's 16," Laura said.

"Yes, and that didn't stop her during the last thunderstorm." His tone was resigned.

Now it was Laura's turn to sigh. But she was smiling.

Her kids were her everything. She would never turn down the chance to cuddle with them during a storm or just spend time with them. Luckily, neither of her kids seemed to mind spending time with their parents. Even though he was 19 and starting his own life, Benny was always working with Joe on the farm. Joe never made him. Benny just wanted to. He enjoyed fixing the equipment with his dad. Laura knew Joe was excited to spend Sunday putting the new part on the tractor with Benny. Tess still spent just as much time with Laura. She loved to help in the kitchen and was becoming quite the good cook. Maybe they could have Ruby over and do some baking tomorrow after church while Benny and Joe fixed the tractor.

Lost in her own happy thoughts of spending the next day with her family, Laura didn't see the car from the other side of the interstate lose control and come across the median. It was a pretty big median and most of it had guard rails or geographic terrain that would've made it near impossible for a car to get across, but there were some small sections here and there that had no barriers. Joe and Laura were driving by such a section right now. Most cars on 81 average about 80 mph in speed despite the 65 mph speed limit. The car had the momentum needed to get across the median and land on the other side in oncoming traffic.

It landed right in front of Joe and Laura's four-door F-150 truck. The last thing they saw were the car's headlights blinding them. Joe didn't even have time to brake before hitting the car head on. The last sounds they heard were breaking glass and crunching metal. And their last thoughts were of their kids waiting for them to come home.

# *Chapter 1*

# TURNING POINT

*"I know there is no straight road, No straight road in this world, Only a giant labyrinth, Of intersecting crossroads."*

— Federico García Lorca

T he strong aroma that only an onion can make permeated the air around me as I chopped and diced. I brushed the tears off my face with a somewhat now grungy looking shirt sleeve. Usually, an onion didn't make me cry like a two-year-old but a dozen onions, I was no match for.

"Tess, Cass is here." The warning from one of the hosting staff was loud enough to be heard over the constant clatter and bang of the busy kitchen. Inwardly, I groaned. Outwardly, everyone else in the kitchen groaned.

"Why tonight?" I mumbled.

Two kitchen staff, one server, one hostess, and Vito Pagano, the head restaurant manager and owner of The Olive Tree, had been knocked down hard with the flu for nearly two weeks; me and the rest of the restaurant staff were running around like mad trying to cover for them. I joined The Tree as it came to be known when I was fresh out of college and the restaurant was just getting started. Now, I was the assistant restaurant manager under Vito. A small, yet high-end Italian restaurant, The Tree was finally starting to make a profit and hold its own in the extremely competitive Northern Virginia market.

Cassio, or Cass, provided Vito funding that he needed to get the restaurant off the ground and keep the doors open when COVID struck. But that money came with a steep price. He gets 20 percent of any revenue for the next 10 years or until the money that he invested is paid back with interest. Whichever comes first. It wouldn't be so bad if he was a silent partner, but he had a habit of showing up, usually at the worst times, to make sure the restaurant was performing to his standards. Though, he had never worked in a restaurant in his life so some of those standards were somewhat questionable.

Cass was also Vito's older brother.

"Luis, I'm heading out front," I yelled to the head chef who was stirring sauce with one hand and sauteing chicken cutlets with the other. I prayed nightly that Luis did not catch the flu because we would be sunk. "Good luck with that boss," he said with his characteristic grin.

I quickly washed my hands and went to greet Cass and see what he wanted tonight. "Please let him not be a colossal prick tonight," I mumbled as I exited the kitchen.

"Tess, we need to talk, now," Cass said, stomping toward me like a man on a mission as soon as I entered the busy waiting area at the front of the restaurant.

"Okay, come on back into Vito's office. We can talk there." I tried to quickly back out of the way so he didn't run me over.

I went into Vito's office with Cass on my heels. Once he was in and sitting down, I quietly took a deep breath and closed the door.

"I've been checking the website and there has been a wait, usually for well over 30 minutes, every night this week," Cass said angrily. "That waiting area is full at 5pm on a Thursday night. What are you doing here Tess?! How many people went to The Olive Garden because the wait at The Olive Tree was crazy long?!" He leaned forward getting in my face and stabbing his finger down on Vito's desk.

I put my hands up to create some space between us. I didn't touch him, but I did try to create some physical space and get him to back off.

"Cass, we are short staffed. Half of the restaurant is out sick. Everyone has been holding down their position while also covering other positions all week."

He glared at me. "I knew you were too young and inexperienced for this job. I told Vito he was making a mistake making you the second in command. This proves it. It's all well and good to keep a business going during the good times, but your good people shine when the chips are down."

He got up from the chair and opened the office door. Turning back, he pointed his finger at me. "Your shine has worn off." Then he left, slamming the door, on his way out.

With shaking hands and fresh tears threatening to spill down my cheeks, I stood up and tried to get my emotions under control. Was I going to be fired? Cass was always an asshole to everyone, including Vito, but he had never threatened my job before. I would get through tonight; once the restaurant was closed, I would call Vito. He was the exact opposite of his brother. Passionate about cooking with a smile for everyone and an easy way about him that made you feel comfortable and at home, he was the best boss in the world and the closest thing I had to a friend in my life. Feeling marginally better, I took one last deep breath and headed out of the office and back into the hustle and bustle of the restaurant.

Four hours later, things were finally starting to slow down. Closing time was at 10pm and it couldn't happen fast enough tonight. I was worn out from the busy, hectic week and then dealing with Cass and his tirade tonight. Taking a break, I got a glass of Diet Coke and went to go sit in Vito's office to start adding up the night's receipts. With any luck, I may be able to finish and get home by midnight.

Thirty minutes later, the forgotten glass of Diet Coke was dripping condensation all over Vito's desk as I focused on going over the schedule for tomorrow to make sure we were able to cover everyone who was out.

"Hey, Vito, welcome back. Feeling better man?" I heard Luis say. I didn't catch Vito's reply, but it must have been brief because he was in the office seconds later.

"Hey Vito, you're here! I didn't expect you for at least another day or two," I exclaimed. I stood up to move out from the back of the desk and let him have his chair, but he waived me down while he closed the door behind him.

The elation I had felt a minute ago started to seep out of me as I registered the look on his face.

He sank down into the chair in front of me. "Tess, there's no easy way to say this..." He stopped talking, leaving the sentence unfinished, and stood up from the chair. He started pacing the office back and forth and running his fingers through his dark hair.

I could feel my heart breaking as I realized what was happening. My stomach was in knots. "Cass wants you to fire me," I said barely above a whisper.

Vito stopped pacing and faced me.

"Damn it!" he shouted and kicked the desk. "Cass is the biggest asshole in the history of assholes. He didn't give me money because he wanted to help me start my dream and get it off the ground. He didn't even do it to make money. He did it so he had something he could hold over me. So, he could control me like he tries to control everyone in his life," he shouted.

I sat there quietly and listened. I knew everything Vito was saying was true. Cass thought his money bought him the right to control everyone around him.

Unfortunately, he seemed to be right.

Vito sat back down in the chair. He hung his head, looking down at the desk. "If I don't let you go, he's going to invoke some clause in the contract that requires me to pay back all the money he invested, with interest, in the next 30 days. It's some clause that he put in there if the restaurant is being mismanaged, he is allowed to collect all the funding he gave me. Apparently, he is the one who gets to judge if it is being mismanaged. I'm sorry."

The sounds of the restaurant bled through the closed door. The kitchen staff and servers were joking around with each other. The stress of the day was starting to fade as the last of the guests finished their meals and left. I stared at my dripping glass of Diet Coke, unable to form words. I finally looked across the desk at Vito. He was sitting on the edge of the chair with his elbows on his knees and head in his hands, staring at the floor, completely dejected. His pose triggered a flash of a memory from long ago that I quickly stuffed back in the far reaches of my mind to be forgotten again.

I slowly stood up from Vito's chair and came around the desk to put my hand on his shoulder.

"It's okay Vito. I understand. There's nothing you can do."

He turned his head in my direction and the complete misery he felt shown all over his face. Being forced to do this was killing a piece of his soul. Unfortunately, I didn't know how to make it any better for him except to leave.

I grabbed my purse and coat that I had thrown in the office haphazardly earlier in the day, squeezed behind the chair Vito was sitting in and quietly slipped out the office door. Afraid that I would completely fall apart if I had to talk to anyone, I slipped through the bar and out through the front. The waiting area was thankfully empty since the doors were locked to any new guests tonight. In a haze, I walked the three blocks to my metro station and waited for the next train.

Luckily, my hours allowed me to miss the worst of the Metro congestion, so there were plenty of empty seats for me to choose from when the train arrived. Despite working in a busy restaurant, I wasn't a fan of crowds or people really. For the most part, I tried to avoid them. I guess that would be easier now that I was fired. Leaning my head against the window, I stuck my hand in my pockets and found my cellphone. I hadn't even thought about it when I left. Thankfully, it was in my coat. I pulled it out absently and checked the screen, not expecting to see anything. Normally, I only got texts or calls about work, so I was a little surprised to see notifications of two missed calls and a waiting text message from my brother.

I heard from Benny occasionally. He tried to keep in touch with me, but I hadn't spoken to him for a long time. I couldn't remember the last time I talked to him. But two missed calls and a text couldn't mean good things. With a little trepidation, I opened my brother's text.

*Hey Tess, I hope things are going okay for you. I hate to tell you this over text, but you aren't answering your phone. Leigh passed away. The doctors are saying it was an aneurysm. She collapsed at work on Tuesday and she never woke up. Call me if you have a chance. Her family is working on funeral arrangements. I think they would love to see you there.*

My grandmother used to babysit to make a living when I was a kid. Leigh was one of the kids she used to watch along with me and Benny and probably half the rest of the kids in Crossroads, VA. Leigh and I were inseparable. She was my best friend. We liked to tell people that didn't know better we were sisters. Though with her fire engine red, curly hair and my dark brown, straight-as-an-arrow hair, I'm pretty sure no one believed us.

I hadn't seen her since the last time she visited me at college years ago. We were both finishing our senior year. Since then, I had reduced our contact to a couple of phone calls on birthdays and some posts on Facebook.

Everything that happened tonight faded to the background as memories of Leigh flooded my brain. Weirdly, I didn't feel anything. It was like my whole emotional grid shut down. I watched through the window as the train pulled into my stop. I got up and waited for the doors to open and let me out into the world. On auto pilot, I walked the five blocks to my apartment. After getting inside, I locked the door behind me and dropped my purse, coat and phone on the floor where I stood.

I looked around at the bare white walls of the studio apartment. It was a nondescript place to live, in a high rise building in Arlington, VA. Calling it a home would be overselling it. It felt like living in a hotel. A bland hotel with no character. But, character cost money, especially in Arlington.

I finally moved away from the door and sat on the edge of my bed, staring at the beige carpeted floor. My thoughts were eerily absent. I should be thinking about Leigh or even the loss of my job, the only thing I really had going for me in my life, but nothing would stick.

My phone buzzed, laying on the floor, with the rest of my stuff. Reluctantly, I stood up and walked the ten feet to get it. Staring at it a second, I picked it up off the floor. It was another text from Benny.

*Did you get my text?*

I texted back yes. Nothing more.

*Are you coming home for the funeral?*

I ignored that one. Picking up my coat and purse off the floor, I dropped them on the bed and went into the kitchen. I stared into the refrigerator like something would magically appear that would make me feel like eating. Giving up on that, I moved to the small hall closet that doubled as my pantry and stared in there for a few minutes.

At some point, my gaze landed on a box of trash bags and finally my thoughts settled onto a plan of action. Grabbing the trash bags, I pulled one out and started stuffing clothes in it.

Three house later, after making endless trips to my old car in the underground garage, I had crammed my car trunk and backseat full of my belongings. Luckily, my apartment had come furnished, so I could leave all the big stuff behind.

Sitting in the front seat, I pulled up the email app on my phone and emailed the building rental office. My lease only had one more month left and any living space was always in high demand in this area. My apartment would probably be filled by the weekend. Throwing my cellphone on the passenger seat, I put the car in gear and headed out of the garage. I had already dropped my keys and garage access card in the night drop box in the building lobby on my last trip into the garage.

On some level, I knew I was acting rashly. Still, at 3:00 a.m. I pulled out of the garage and headed west on interstate 66.

# Chapter 2

# NO PLACE LIKE HOME

*"Why do you go away? So that you can come back. So that you can see the place you came from with new eyes and extra colors. And the people there see you differently, too. Coming back to where you started is not the same as never leaving."*

— Terry Pratchett, A Hat Full of Sky

A s I got closer to my exit, my emotions were all over the map. My anxiety about going back home and my grief about Leigh battled with my desire – no requirement – for coffee. How people go through life without coffee has always baffled me. I would never understand it. At minimum, a cup in the morning is a necessity. A large cup. Moments later, I was off the exit and pulling into a gas station. After filling my car at the pump, I went inside where the aroma of fresh coffee hit me as soon as I opened the door.

Grabbing the biggest cup on the counter, I filled it as full as possible while still leaving room for a little cream. Taking a tentative first sip to test the temperature, I walked the aisles, looking for something edible. There really isn't a decent breakfast to be found in a gas station convenience store. "Hello, sugar." I grabbed a box of chocolate donuts.

The chilly spring air hit me as soon as I left the store and goosebumps instantly formed on my arms. Quickly getting into my car, I cranked the engine and took a big gulp from my cup. As the car heated up, I enjoyed the warmth of the coffee going through me. As it got warmer, I put the car in reverse, took my foot off the brake and drifted backward out of the parking spot. I stopped and stared out at the road while my stomach did somersaults.

A loud, somewhat angry-sounding horn jerked me out of my reverie and back to the task at hand. In the rearview mirror, I saw a work truck waiting to get out and get on with the day. I took a deep breath, accepted the inevitable, and made a right out of the parking lot and headed for Crossroads.

Within a couple of miles, the houses began to get further apart, broken up by farms and fields with cows standing in the early morning light. Sites and houses that I had known in my past, spent time in, passed by in my periphery. Crossroads was one of many map dot small towns that were scattered all over Virginia. I drove through the tiny town square and made a left at the intersecting roads in the middle of town that gave Crossroads its name.

Despite driving slowly, it didn't take long before a familiar, and somewhat misplaced, weeping willow tree came into view just to the left up ahead. The tree did not fit in with its surroundings and no one knows how it got there but it was good way of telling people how to find my brother's house. I hung a left and listened to my tires crunch up the long gravel driveway while doing a quick search for Benny's Jeep. It wasn't here. My nerves calmed a little and I let out the breath I didn't realize I was holding. He was at work. I put the car in park and stared at the house. It was a dark blue two-story A-frame with a freshly painted white front porch and matching white shutters framing the windows.

It was a stark contrast between now and my first view of the house years ago when Benny first brought me to it.

"I'm sorry we had to sell the farm Tess," Benny had said quietly as he drove us to our new home eight years earlier. I stared out the passenger window and didn't respond.

"The house may need some fixing up, but I'll work on it," he continued after he realized I wasn't going to say anything. "Maybe we can fix it up together."

I shrugged my shoulders and continued staring out the window. I didn't care.

The rest of the drive was done in silence. Benny turned the car up a long driveway that was more dirt and weeds than gravel. Except for a bizarre weeping willow when we first turned in, the driveway wove through pine and oak trees until it ended in a clearing with a decrepit little house covered in chipped white paint. Crumbling concrete stairs led up to a sagging front porch. A rickety screen door that hung off the hinges completed the whole blissful picture. Home sweet home.

"It will get better," Benny said.

I didn't respond.

Turning off the ignition, I sat back in my car seat with a sigh as the memory washed over me, Sipping my coffee, I stared at the little house. I had to hand it to him, Benny brought life back to the house. Most people, myself included, would've bull dozed it.

Opening the creaking door of the Toyota, I walked up the smooth concrete stairs to the wooden porch and used my key to let myself in. The house wasn't big and wouldn't stand out to most people, but my brother was good on his word. He had fixed it up and maintained it well. The stairs to the second floor, and my bedroom, were right inside the entrance. With a little trepidation, I headed upstairs with my backpack that had a change of clothes and some toiletries. What if it wasn't my room anymore? Why had that thought not occurred to me until now? And why did it matter? I wasn't moving back in permanently.

Reaching the top of the stairs, I walked down the short hallway and into the bedroom... and back in time.

Everything was just as I had left it.

It was a small room with sloping ceilings so you could only stand up straight in the dead center. It was just big enough to fit a full-size bed, but there was a big closet. Closet may not be the right word. It was an attic like area that had never been finished. My brother had run some electricity to it, strung white Christmas lights throughout the rafters, and put up hooks and closet railings to hang my clothes on. My small desk and chair, plus some bookshelves, occupied one side and a dresser was on the other. A mirror hung on the back of the door. There was a fan for the summer when it was sweltering hot and a space heater for the winter when it was freezing cold.

Flipping the switch just inside the door, I smiled as everything was illuminated. He hadn't changed a thing, though I hadn't been back since college graduation, and that visit was just a pit stop on my way to Northern Virginia. I hadn't even been back for the holidays.

Sitting my backpack down on the chair, I pulled out a change of clothes and set them on the desk. My old terry-cloth robe hung on a hook by the dresser. It was a little dusty maybe, but I could still smell the Downy fabric softener. Benny and I always washed our clothes in original Tide and April Fresh Downy. It was what mom had used. Even so, our clothes didn't smell like they did when mom cleaned them.

After a shower, I went out to the car and started unloading everything. I'm not sure when I decided to move back in with my brother. Not that I had many options at this point. After at least fifteen trips down the stairs to my car and then back up again - the whole time telling myself that this was only temporary - my room, that was nice and neat less than an hour ago, was now crammed full of my stuff.

"When did I get so much crap?"

The crunch of a vehicle driving over the gravel driveway came through the open window mixed with the lyrics of an old Pearl Jam song. My stomach did a somersault again.

Why is Benny home now?

Benny is a mechanic in our uncle's auto shop. He started working there in high school and continued after graduation. College never appealed to him. He'd always loved fixing things and would often help our dad around our small farm when he was younger. In his spare time, he bought old cars, trucks, and motorcycles and restored them. But he didn't just restore. He improved and turned something that was dying a slow death from rust and decay into something beautiful.

I heard the front door open and Benny's deep voice calling up the stairs. "Tess?"

"Yes, it's just me," I said as I came down to meet him.

His face lit up into a big smile when he saw me, and he grabbed me into a hug. Any nerves or apprehension I had fled, replaced by an overwhelming sense of guilt.

"I didn't know if you would want to come back for the funeral," he said.

I ran my hand through my long hair, scooping my few wispy bangs out of my eyes. Looking at my brother, it hit me how long I had stayed away. He looked pretty much the same, but there were subtle signs that he was getting older. At 27, his face had the start of a few lines around the eyes and mouth. No doubt, I contributed to some of those lines. But it wasn't just his physical appearance. Benny always had a maturity that went beyond his years and that only got stronger with age. Quiet by nature, he was never Mr. Popular in high school, but he had a few close friends that stuck by both of us through a lot of dark days. We both had the same blue eyes and dark brown hair, though Benny always kept his military short just like our dad. He had a strong build from long hours doing manual labor for most of his life. Neither one of us was short nor tall. We weren't winning any beauty contests, but we didn't look like we'd been beaten with an ugly stick either.

"Well, I kind of moved back in. Temporarily," I added hastily. I looked at the floor, the walls, anything but my brother, who has always seen straight through me. He was quiet and when I finally looked at him, I saw him staring at me in thought. Then he just shrugged his shoulders.

"Need any help with your stuff?" He walked past me into the small kitchen at the back of the house.

Thinking he was going to want some sort of explanation; it took me a minute to regroup and respond to his question. "No, I didn't have much, and I've already put it up in my room," I said, following him to the kitchen.

I sat down at the small kitchen table while Benny made some coffee. The kitchen cabinets were still the same white color Benny and a couple of his friends had painted them when we first moved in. Some of mom's colorful pottery that she had made were scattered along the countertops. The kitchen was small and could use some updating, but it was clean and cozy.

"What are you doing home so early?" I asked.

"I took today off to take care of some things."

Well, that was vague.

I watched as Benny went into one of the cabinets and pulled down two coffee mugs and then to the refrigerator for the cream. And for some reason, watching him do this normal activity of making coffee, it occurred to me that my brother has his own life. After devoting a significant portion of his twenties to taking care of me, making sure I graduated high school and then college, he could think of himself. Until now, when I came back home and moved back in without so much as a heads up to him. I mentally smacked myself on the forehead.

"Have you had breakfast yet?" Benny asked.

His question snapped me out of my train of thought. "Does gas station coffee and chocolate donuts count?"

He rolled his eyes. "Do you want me to fix you some eggs?"

And now, he's going to start taking care of me again. Not this time. If I was staying, temporarily, I could help him. That would be the silver lining to getting canned from my job.

"No thanks, I'm not that hungry. Do you need any help with anything? You said you took today off to take care of some things."

He was quiet for a second. "I'm working on something. It's still in the early stages, so I haven't been talking about it a lot yet."

"You never talk about anything a lot," I joked.

He smiled. "Haha," he said dryly. "Maybe I talk, and you just never listen."

We could bicker like this all day and often did when we were growing up. To put an end to it, I closed my mouth and waited for him to spill the beans.

"Uncle Rob is retiring. He asked me if I wanted to take over the shop," Benny said.

My heart broke a little at the mention of Uncle Rob. I was scared to death to run into him. Because I didn't know how he would react. If he would forgive me. I had broken his heart.

"Wow, you've been working there forever," I said as Benny put a cup of coffee in front of me and sat down with his own. "That's great if it's what you want. Is it what you want?" I asked.

Benny nodded. "Yes, but I've got ideas for changing it a bit. Kind of making it my own. I will need to take out a business loan and probably do a much better job of networking and marketing to get my name out there. Not exactly a strength of mine."

He ran his hand over his head and looked a little panicked and overwhelmed by the whole thing. This was unfamiliar territory for me. My brother had been my rock for many years. He always seemed to know what to do. Before our parents died, we were close. Then, after their deaths, he became my guardian and raised me. He was only nineteen years old. His life was just getting started, and he got stuck with raising his emotionally traumatized sixteen-year-old sister who had turned her back on the world. He didn't complain. At least, not where I could hear it. He handled everything from our parent's funeral arrangements to making sure we had a place to live when our small farm was foreclosed on. Maybe it was time for me to step up and be there for him.

# Chapter 3

# MEMORIES CRASH

*"The world breaks everyone and after, many are stronger at the broken places."*

— Ernest Hemingway

Benny had to run out and do some more errands, so I went back upstairs to clean up the mess I had made of my room. After getting things organized enough that I could live with it, I went downstairs to see how much food was in the house. I could at least buy some groceries after moving back in without so much as a phone call to make sure my room was still available. I knew it would be. My brother would always have a home for me. That was just the way he was.

As I searched through the cabinets and refrigerator, my phone rang. I didn't recognize the number, but it was local. Finally, on the fourth ring, I answered it and put it on speaker.

"Hello."

"Hi Tess? This is Leigh's Aunt Trudy."

"Oh, hi, I..." I stammered while dropping the canned vegetables I had been sorting through. "Sorry," I tried to speak over the noise of the can clattering to the kitchen floor. "How are you doing?"

"I'm hanging in there." Her voice sounded tired, actually more than tired. She sounded utterly exhausted.

"How are Mr. And Mrs. Shay?" I asked quietly as I sat down at the kitchen table.

"Honestly, devastated and barely functioning." Her voice choked up.

In all of my packing, driving, and unpacking, I had mentally blocked thinking about Leigh's death. How young she was, how it would affect her family, how I felt about it, but listening to Leigh's aunt trying to control her tears brought it all to the surface.

"How are you holding up?" she asked me after a moment.

"Hanging in there too."

She didn't need to know and could probably care less that immediately after getting fired and hearing about Leigh's death, I packed up my apartment and moved back in with my brother. Besides, if I was being true to myself, I couldn't blame all my actions on Leigh's death or even being fired. It might have been the spark that lit the fire, but it had been smoldering for a long time. Losing Leigh and my job so suddenly has pushed everything I've been missing to the surface, and I have nothing to cover it up with anymore. No hectic job to focus on and no comfort in the thought that I would always have Leigh.

"Are you going to make it to the funeral?" she asked. "It's next Saturday."

"Yes, of course. I'm actually in town now and am going to her parent's house this afternoon. Do you know if they need anything or if there is anything I can do to help?"

Trudy was silent.

"Trudy?" I prompted.

"They wanted me to ask you to do the eulogy."

The eulogy. My breath caught in my chest, and a swirl of contradicting emotions rushed through me. Terror. But also, love and an overwhelming sense of gratitude that they would trust me to speak at the funeral. And finally, all of it was buried under the immense loss that hit me like an avalanche. The mental dam I had put up to block my feelings broke.

"Yes," I whispered. "I can write the eulogy."

"Thank you, Tess. It really means a lot to them and me, and I know it would mean a lot to Leigh."

"It's an honor. If you need anything, let me know. Please."

"I will. Talk to you soon. Thanks again, Tess."

She hung up, and I sat there clutching my phone and trying to get my scattered thoughts in line. I stared at the small kitchen table. It was a round wooden table that used to be in my grandma's house. She fed all of us kids at it when she was babysitting. My uncle had it in his basement since grandma died and gave it to Benny to use in this house after our parents died.

Leigh and I ate at this table more times than I could count. Some of my earliest memories of us together are sitting at this table eating and laughing, coloring, playing checkers, and telling little girl secrets. So many memories I hadn't thought of in years.

Blowing out a long breath, I stood up and made myself put one foot in front of the other and go upstairs. My old journal hid in the wall behind my desk inside my makeshift closet, forgotten for years. I stopped writing in it the day my parents died. I was afraid of what would come out of me. But I also couldn't throw it away.

I went back downstairs to the little kitchen table, sat down, opened my journal to a blank page, and began to write.

*I've known Leigh for as long as I can remember. She was always at my grandma's house when I went to visit. We were instantly best friends, even though we were total opposites. She was the pretty, girly one that liked to paint her nails and wear her hair down. She was also incredibly sweet and kind. And tolerant. She certainly put up with me, probably more than she should. Even though it wasn't her thing, she would climb trees, play ball, and get dirty, because that was what I wanted to do. Looking back, we were always doing what I wanted to do. Rarely did I play dolls or dress up like she would want...*

I sat back in the chair and gently laid my pen down across the page. One paragraph. I felt like my heart was being torn apart. It wasn't the memories of our childhood together breaking my heart. We had not seen each other for at least two years, and it was my fault. She had tried to keep in touch and kept trying to make plans. I was always too busy. Too busy in a life that didn't even hold any happiness for me. I had checked out on Leigh, and everyone really, in high school after my parents died.

I took a deep breath and closed the journal, shoving it in my purse. I needed to put a lid back on my grief for now and get my emotions under control. Grabbing my purse, I went outside and got in my car. I sat in the driver's seat and stared out the window. My head was a jumbled mess in one sense, but also completely blank. I couldn't decide which thought running through my head I needed to focus on, so I didn't focus on any of them. Turning the key, I started the car and its trusty engine roared to life. Sending a silent prayer of thanks, I turned around and drove down the long driveway. At the end of it, on auto pilot, I turned left.

A few short minutes later, I stopped in the middle of the road and looked out the window. Without thinking about where I was going or why, my natural instincts took over and I found myself in front of Jack's house.

Sighing, I laid my head on the steering wheel. Why was I here?

He probably wasn't home. God, I silently prayed, please don't let him be home. Simultaneously, my stomach was doing somersaults at the thought of seeing him.

Jack's family owned the farm next to the little house that Benny rented and eventually bought when our parents died and we lost our farm. Whereas our farm had been small and more of a side job for my parents than anything else, the Hallowell farm was a business. They had deals to supply meat, chicken, and produce to large commercial food distributors. Running a large farm and keeping distributors happy is a stressful business. The Hallowells earned every cent they made with a lot of blood, sweat, and tears running that farm year after year.

I smiled a little as I remembered my first encounter with Jack on our elementary school playground. I was bored with the swings and the monkey bars, so I wandered over to where some of the boys were playing a thrilling game of kickball.

"Hey, can I play?" I asked the first boy I came to.

He looked at me and laughed. "We don't want to play with some little girl," he responded snidely. Some of the other boys nearby laughed too but most of them looked nervous. I wasn't sure why but didn't really feel like figuring it out right then.

My face immediately felt hot with embarrassment. I could feel tears welling up in my eyes, but I shut it down. I am not crying in front of a bunch of stupid boys.

"What? Scared I might beat you?" I replied with my own sneer.

"Yeah right," he said with a snort. "Look, this is a boys' game. Go play somewhere else." He was no longer laughing as he got up in my face. I took a step back. I had an older brother and we argued sometimes but he never acted like that towards me. Kickball Boy was scary.

"Why are you such a jerk Anders? Back off her," said another boy as he rushed over and stood between us. I peeked around my savior to see Kickball Boy, or Anders I guess is his name, back up a step.

"What? Is she your little girlfriend or something Jack?" Anders replied.

Jack didn't take the bait. He just stood there and stared at Anders. I noticed no one was playing kickball anymore as they watched Jack and Anders.

"Got nothing to say? Cat got your tongue? She's just a stupid little girl. What are you, second grade?" he asked looking at me. I didn't respond. This kid seemed a little unhinged and I didn't want to cause anymore trouble for the boy who had come to help me.

"Anders, we're playing a game of kickball at recess, not the Super Bowl. You don't need to be such a jerk because someone else wants to play. I say let her play and whoever doesn't like it can shut his pie hole," Jack said looking directly at Anders.

Anders had the red face now. I knew he wanted to punch Jack, but I didn't think he had the guts. Most bullies don't when someone stands up to them.

Proving my point, Anders threw the kickball down and stormed off.

"You okay?" Jack asked as he turned to face me.

I smiled at him. "Yeah, I'm fine. Thanks for coming over here. I didn't mean to ruin the game," I said.

"You didn't ruin anything. Anders has always been a butthead. Come on, there's still a few minutes left of recess, let's go play," he said as one of the boys threw the kickball to him.

I smiled and jogged next to him over to where the other boys were taking their positions, without Anders now.

"I'm Tess," I said to Jack.

Jack smiled. "Jack Hallowell. Nice to meet you, Tess."

From that day on, I sought Jack out on the playground until he left me behind at elementary school and moved up to the middle school. He was a year ahead of me in school. Eventually, our families became acquainted and then became friends. Jack and I stayed friends through the awkward middle school years and on into the angst-filled high school years. Until, one summer, we became something more.

The summer before my sophomore year and Jack's junior year was almost like any other in the sense that every free moment, Jack, me, Leigh, and sometimes Benny and Jack's brothers were hanging out, four-wheeling, or going to the lake for a swim. It was easier now since a couple of the kids in the group had their driver's licenses and could pick up whoever needed a lift instead of nagging our parents for a ride.

One night, we were all camping out at my parent's farm. This was something we did often in the spring and summer, ever since we were kids. Usually, everyone's parents were there too, hanging out by the fire and "shooting the shit" as my dad would say, until we were ready to go to our tents and sleep. This night, the last camp out before school started back up, the parents turned in early and so did most of the friends. It had been a busy day on the farms digging up potatoes, picking the last of the green beans, and getting things ready for the fall. People were tired.

Jack and I were sitting by the fire, just the two of us. Things had been feeling different between him and me for some time. Really, ever since I started high school, though neither of us would acknowledge nor talk about it. He dated some other girls here and there and I had short-lived relationships with some other boys, but not anything serious for either of us.

Sharing a blanket on the ground, we were sitting next to each other, leaning against the logs my parents had put around the fire pits for seating. We were staring into the fire, not talking, when his hand drifted to mine. I looked down as he slid his fingers down my palm and between my fingers. We both closed our fingers over each other's hands at the same time. I looked over at him and met his gaze. He always had the prettiest hazel eyes. Then he leaned over and kissed me. It was soft and a little hesitant. I opened my mouth just a little, and the kiss turned a bit more passionate. It was the best kiss of my young life.

A tear rolled down my cheek and dripped onto the steering wheel as I sat in my car in the middle of the road remembering how it all started. I stared at his parent's house, lost in my memories when a car horn broke my train of thought. I looked in my review mirror and was about to wave out the window in apology when I saw who was in the truck behind me.

Jack.

# Chapter 4

# REBUILDING

*"There is an ocean of silence between us... and I am drowning in it."*

— Ranata Suzuki

I had a split second to debate turning off the road and going down the Hallowell family's long driveway or driving away as fast as my little rusty old Toyota would take me.

I was done with running, so I turned down the driveway and pulled to a stop in front of the Hallowell's farmhouse. Jack pulled in next to me but didn't get out of the truck. He was probably having the same debate in his head I just did, get out of the truck or back up and drive away as fast as possible. After at least a full minute, he opened his truck door and got out.

He didn't look a lot different from the last time I saw him back in high school. Same dark wavy hair that was curling on the ends. He would need to get a haircut soon. I used to cut it for him. Who does it now? He wore a blue t-shirt that showed his muscular arms and chest and no-nonsense jeans that showed wear from work and age rather than any kind of fashion statement. I looked down and stared at his work boots as he came around the truck and walked toward me. It took everything in me to lift my head and look him in the eyes. It wasn't until I did, that I noticed he had aged. He had aged well. He still looked good, but it was evident stress and years had left an imprint on him.

"Hey," I tried to say, but it came out as more of a whisper. My voice chose this moment to go on a retreat.

He looked at me for a minute like he didn't know if he wanted to hug me or throw me in the pen to the pigs. I wouldn't have blamed him if he did.

"Hi Tess," he said flatly. "I wondered if I would run into you. If you would bother coming back for Leigh's funeral."

That stung. Unfortunately, it stung because it was deserved. I had to look away from him for a minute to take a breath and hope my voice made a reappearance.

"I'm staying at Benny's. I actually moved back in."

A look of surprise crossed his face, and I thought, maybe a little happiness. But that last part might have been wishful thinking. To his credit, he didn't pry, though he probably had a million questions. Or maybe he didn't. Maybe he was beyond caring. That happens when you push people away long enough. I spent so much time wallowing in my own issues and misery after my parents died, I didn't have time for anyone else. Not Leigh, not Jack, not even Benny.

Jack was the one I pushed away the hardest. I was 16 when my parents died and in my junior year of high school. Jack was a senior and spent most of his senior year trying to support me through a terrible time in my life and hold our relationship together. But it takes two people to make a relationship work. All the effort in the world can't make it happen when its all coming from only one side of the coin.

After an awkward moment of silence, the manners Jack's mom drilled into her boys seeped through. "Would you like to come in?" he asked, albeit somewhat begrudgingly. It was like his mom was sitting on his shoulder nagging him to be polite no matter what.

"Sure," I said before I could think it through. I knew he wanted me to leave. But I had this overwhelming desire to make things right between us. Or, at least better than they are now. We may never be friends, but anything would be better than the awkwardness we were having right now.

He led the way up the big front porch into the old two-level farmhouse that had been in their family for more than a hundred years. The family had changed and added onto it over the years, but you could still see the original framework and brick. This house had character. We went through the foyer and living room to the back, where the big farm kitchen was located. Two smaller porches were off either side of the kitchen, which spanned the whole back of the house.

Jack poured us some tea his mom made and kept in the fridge at all times. Hell would freeze over before Jenny Hallowell let the tea pitcher go empty. I sipped the drink and felt the coolness go down my throat. I hadn't had tea like this in years. It was cold and sweet and mixed with a splash of lemonade. Perfect. I missed this.

Jack and I sat at the long wooden table that showed its age, but that's what made it beautiful. All the dark marks and indents in the wood told the story of years of family dinners, holiday baking, home-work sessions, art projects, card games, all the normal things that families do together every day without thinking about how special it is and how fleeting.

"I'm sorry," I said quietly.

He looked at me, and after a moment, he nodded. "I know," he said.

I'm not sure if he knew I was apologizing for everything—the way I handled my parents' deaths, pushing everyone away, leaving. The list was long. I used their deaths as an excuse to fall apart and forget everything they ever taught me about personal strength, accountability, and just being a decent human being.

"Leigh's parents asked me to do the eulogy."

"I thought they might," he replied. "I went to see them yesterday, but only saw Mrs. Shay. She asked me if I thought you would do it. I told them the old you would do the eulogy in a heartbeat. But I wasn't sure about the girl who left here and never looked back."

Sipping my tea, I remained quiet. I didn't know what to say to that because I understood where he was coming from. To try to explain away or rationalize all my behavior before I left town would be disingenuous. Not wanting to sit in awkward silence, I changed the subject.

"Benny's taking over the garage. Uncle Rob is semi-retiring. I think he's going to stay on part-time or as much as he feels like anyway to help Benny out, especially at first."

"Wow," Jack said. "I haven't seen much of Benny lately. Maybe that's why. I had no idea. That's pretty huge. Is that what he wants?"

"I only talked to him about it for a few minutes this morning, but I think so. He said he has some changes he wants to make. Honestly, he seemed a bit overwhelmed. I've never seen him unsure of what to do next," I said. "He always knows what to do."

Jack looked at me. "Benny doesn't always know what to do," he said, clearly annoyed with me. "You are growing up. We are growing up. We're adults now. Part of being an adult is realizing the people you thought had all the answers are human like everyone else. I used to think my parents knew everything. I never questioned it. But, now I'm an adult and they are treating me like an adult, so I see the part of the process I never had insight into as a kid. They sit and talk for hours and do research for days, weeks, and months to figure out if something is a good business decision. Now, I see the aftermath when they make the wrong choice. They kept us away from all of that as kids. Benny did the same for you. I'm sure he didn't always have the answers after your parents died and when he was trying to raise you, but he made sure that part was hidden from you. You needed to know you still had someone to count on."

The cold condensation from the tea glass ran down the glass and through my fingers. Focusing on the cool sensation helped me keep my emotions under control. For the second time today, I realized how much Benny took on and how much I took him for granted.

"I'm going to help him," I said. "Benny doesn't have to do everything on his own. He doesn't have to protect me anymore. I want to help him do this, make this business what he wants it to be."

"So, you are definitely moving back here? For good?" Jack asked.

I hesitated because I didn't know that. And I couldn't promise it.

"No one knows what's going to happen down the road, but I'm here now. Though, in hindsight, I probably should have asked Benny before showing up and moving back in," I said with a little laugh.

"No, he probably would've been insulted if you asked him first. He made that home for you and him. He always wanted you to feel like you had a place to go if you needed it."

All the times I made excuses when Benny asked me to come home for a holiday or birthday ran through my head.

"Why did you come by here?" Jack asked quietly.

It was a valid question. I wasn't entirely sure of the answer. You know how when you are driving and get to work, home, the grocery store—some place you've driven to a million times—and don't remember actually driving there? That was how I ended up at Jack's house.

"I don't know." And that was the God's honest truth. "I'm still trying to wrap my head around Leigh being gone." I stopped and took a deep breath. My chest felt like there was a weight on it. Taking a small sip of tea, I focused on the coolness of the liquid running down my throat.

Jack waited patiently, saying nothing.

"I alienated the people who care about me most. I want to fix that." Until I said it out loud, I really didn't know that reconnecting with everyone I left behind was part of what drove me to come back. "I don't entirely know how, but I'm going to try. For Leigh, I'm going to be there for her family as much as they will have me, and that starts with writing the eulogy. I'm great with writing about us growing up but recent memories are few and far between. Can you think about the past few years? Anything about her that would help me with writing about Leigh, the adult, would be very helpful."

He nodded. "I have a few thoughts."

"Great," I said, standing up. I took my glass to the sink, washed it, and put it in the strainer out of habit. On the notepad that was always next to the refrigerator, I wrote my email address and cell number for him. "Please email me whatever you can think of. Or call... if you want to talk," I said a little hesitantly. I didn't know where I stood with him. If he would even be interested in talking to me anymore.

He nodded but nothing more, so I turned away and left him sitting in the kitchen.

# Chapter 5

# FINDING TESS

*"Things we lose have a way of coming back to us in the end, if not always in the way we expect."*
— JK Rowling, Harry Potter and the Order of the Phoenix

After leaving Jack's, I went to see Leigh's parents. They lived "in town" which was really a tiny neighborhood of houses near the town center of Crossroads. My nerves already felt frayed, and the lack of sleep the night before was undoubtedly not helping. But I couldn't rest until I went to see the Shays.

I slowly brought the car to a stop in front of their small brick home. The sight of the house brought a wave of memories crashing over me. I had spent as much time there as my home growing up. The Shays only had one child. Leigh. Losing my parents was the hardest thing I ever went through; it changed me. But, to lose your only child, I could only imagine the grief the Shays were feeling. For what seemed like the hundredth time in the past day and a half, tears threatened but I held them at bay. My tears would not help The Shays.

"Come on, Tess, pull it together."

The front door opened, and Mrs. Shay stood in the doorway, staring at me. And the emotional dam broke. I opened the car door, ran across the front lawn and threw myself into her arms, sobbing like a three-year-old. She said nothing, but her arms wrapped around me, and her warmth brought comfort. Eventually, my tears slowed down and my breathing became more even, and it finally dawned on me I was supposed to be comforting Mrs. Shay, not the other way around. She led me into the house and shut the front door. We sat down on the couch in the living room. The curtains were drawn and the light was dim. Mr. Shay was nowhere in sight.

"Hi," I said lamely.

"Hi honey," Mrs. Shay responded while handing me some tissues and brushing the hair out of my face. She looked like she had aged twenty years since the last time I saw her. Her normally shiny hair that she always took time to style was dull and unwashed. She wore old jeans and a stained shirt. Her rumpled clothes looked like she had been in them for a couple of days. Normally, Mrs. Shay always wore make-up, no matter what we were doing. Not today.

Not knowing how to start, I brushed her hair back out of her face. She needed help. I wrapped my arms around her and held her the way she held me a few moments ago. She didn't cry; she just laid there on my shoulder and let me rub her back.

"When was the last time you slept?" I asked her quietly.

"I don't know. I can't sit still. But I can't focus on anything to get something done either. I mostly just walk around the house."

She looked and sounded lost.

"Where is Mr. Shay?" I asked.

"In bed." She glanced up the stairs. "He doesn't get out of bed. He just lays there."

I looked around the house. Dishes of food people had brought over covered the dining room table. Some of the food looked like it had been sitting there for some time.

"Mrs. Shay, you need to rest. You are exhausted. Please, go lay down with Mr. Shay. I'll stay here and keep an eye on things and talk to anyone who comes by."

She nodded slowly but didn't make any move to get up, so I stood up from the couch and pulled her to her feet. Taking her by the arm, I led her up the stairs to her bedroom. In the room, Mr. Shay was lying on the bed, on top of the covers. His eyes were open, but it did not seem like they were seeing anything. For a brief second, I wondered if he was alive, but then I saw him blink. That was it. Otherwise, he didn't move or acknowledge our presence. Like Mrs. Shay, his normally neatly combed hair was a mess and didn't look like he had washed it recently. His glasses were on the floor near the wall across from the bed. Luckily, it looked like they didn't break when he apparently threw them across the room.

Guiding Mrs. Shay to the bed the way you would a sleepy child, I pulled back the covers and gently helped her lie down. Walking to the other side of the bed, I tried to get Mr. Shay to move so I could cover him, too. For a minute, he didn't seem to notice that I was nudging his arm, but then he finally turned his head and looked at me.

"Come on Mr. Shay, let me cover you," I said to him quietly.

The bags under his eyes stood out against his pale skin. He didn't fight me when I pulled him to his feet so I could pull back the covers. Still dressed for work, his tie hung loose and crooked around his neck. Guiding him to sit down on the bed, I removed the tie before he laid back down in the same position as before. I pulled the covers over him and picked his glasses up off the floor to put on the nightstand next to the bed.

I prayed they would sleep. Closing the door quietly behind me, I looked down the hall toward Leigh's old room. My chest ached at the thought of going in there. Hanging my head, I debated if I had the strength. It wasn't something that was going to get easier with time, so slowly I walked down the hall. I stopped at the open doorway. The space was exactly the same as when we were in high school.

The walls were pink. As in Barbie pink. She loved it no matter how much I picked on her about it when we were growing up. I skimmed my hand along the top of the old white dresser. I remember when her mom got that dresser. We were young, maybe seven or eight, and at a flea market with Mrs. Shay. Leigh saw it and begged her mom to buy it. I thought the thing would be better used as firewood, but Leigh and her mom saw the potential. So, the three of us somewhat dragged, somewhat carried the heavy dresser all the way to the Shay's old truck and got it in the back. We spent all weekend sanding and painting. When we were done, even I had to admit, it looked pretty good. Leigh loved it.

Same went for her old, wooden sleigh bed. Another flea market find that Leigh and her mom had repurposed and brought back to life. Leigh hated waste and loved to scour flea markets and yard sales for the old and discarded. She had a talent for finding treasure where most of us only saw trash.

I sat down on Leigh's bed. The quilt her grandmother made her when she was a baby covered the bed, along with some throw pillows. The pillows were pink, of course. She had pictures everywhere, most of her family, Jack, and me. Her favorite purse she always used in high school still hung on the back of her desk chair like it was waiting for her to run in and grab it to go shopping.

Tears ran down my face, but I didn't realize it until they dripped onto my hands. Wiping my hands off on my jeans, I stood up and used my sleeves to dry my cheeks. I tiptoed down the hall to Leigh's parents' room and peeked through the door, hoping they were asleep. They faced each other, hands clasped in between them. I quietly closed the door and went back downstairs.

Grabbing some paper from the junk drawer in the kitchen, I wrote a quick note to please not ring the doorbell and taped it to the storm door so there was no missing it. I left the front door cracked and opened the curtains and windows. This way, I would notice if someone came up the walk, and it would also air out the house a bit.

Looking around, I tackled the food on the dining room table first. I wasn't sure if I could salvage any of it. Who knew how long it had been sitting there? There was a lot of food. I hated to get rid of it all, but I would not risk the Shay's getting sick when they finally ate something.

I walked over to the table and couldn't help but smile a little. Mrs. Shay, even under these circumstances, had attached post-it notes to all the food, so she knew who brought it and could return the bowl, pot, or plate. I picked up the closest dish and looked under the tinfoil. A blueberry pie. That should be okay, so I moved it to the credenza by the wall. The next dish was a shepherd's pie that looked like it had been there for some time. I pulled the trash can out of the kitchen and into the dining room and got to work.

I was drying the last dish off and making a neat stack on the table when I felt my phone vibrate in my back pocket. It was an unknown number, but local.

"Hello?"

"Hey."

It was Jack. Every one of my nerves seemed to come alive at the sound of his voice. I really wasn't sure he would ever use it when I left him my phone number. Neither of us said anything for a second, and I knew he was wondering if this was a mistake or even why he called. Before he could think on that for too long, I broke the silence.

"I'm at the Shay's house. They're sleeping, so I'm trying to clean up and keep an eye out for any visitors."

"That's good," he said. "I only saw Mrs. Shay for a minute when I stopped by, and she looked like she was hanging on by a thread."

"She's laying down with Mr. Shay. I'm hoping they sleep through the night. I don't think either of them has slept in days."

He was quiet for another minute, and I was about to say something else to fill the void when he beat me to it.

"Have you eaten dinner?" he asked.

"No, not yet," I said, looking at the clock on the microwave. "Holy crap, it's 6:00 already? Damn, I was going to do some grocery shopping and make dinner for Benny."

"I just passed by the shop," Jack said. "His Jeep is still outside. Why don't you pick up some subs or burgers and I'll get some beers and meet you at your house. I'll go back by the shop and let Benny know, so he comes home for dinner."

Did he not usually come home for dinner? The question ran through my head, but I stopped myself from saying it out loud. Dinner had always been a big deal for my family. It didn't matter if we were eating a full course meal or peanut butter and jelly. There were the occasional exceptions, but for the most part, we always ate dinner together. It was a big deal to my mom and dad. After they were gone, Benny kept it going even though it was just the two of us. I guess there was no reason for Benny to come home for dinner after I left.

Then it hit me what Jack was saying. He wants to come over and have dinner with us?

"Umm, sure, that sounds great," I said. I was trying to keep my tone casual but, on the inside, a hornet's nest was getting worked up like someone just kicked their hive. "I'll see you in about an hour. I need to finish up here and then I'll head out."

"Cool, I'll see you there," he said.

He sounded relaxed. Maybe too relaxed, like it was forced.

I put my phone back in my pocket and tried to focus on wiping down the table and counters. I didn't want to make a big deal about that phone call from Jack. Was he trying to reconnect? He seemed like he could barely tolerate the sight of me at his house earlier.

As I threw all the dirty dish towels I created into the laundry room, my phone vibrated with a text message.

Jack changed his mind was the first thought that popped into my head.

I pulled my phone out of my pocket slowly and looked at the screen, dreading to see Jack's name. But it wasn't Jack. It was Vito, my ex-boss.

*I have an opportunity for you. They need someone soon, so you will have to act fast if you are interested. This would be great for you! Call me as soon as you can.*

# Chapter 6

# OLIVE BRANCHES

*"There is no place like home."*
— L. Frank Baum, The Wonderful Wizard of Oz

I looked in on the Shays one last time before leaving. They were still in the same positions, facing each other and holding hands. My heart broke for them. I left a note that I would be back tomorrow, made sure the house was locked up, and left another note on the door asking people to let them rest and come back at another time.

When I got in my car, I looked at the text from Vito again. As I sat there and let my car warm up, I debated calling him. I liked Vito a lot, but I couldn't pretend that whole experience with Cass and being fired after I had busted my ass helping get that restaurant off the ground and keeping it going when half the place came down with the flu didn't effect me. I definitely never wanted to see or talk to Cass again. And, if I'm being honest with myself, part of me wanted to avoid Vito too.

I guess I should at least hear about this opportunity that would be so great for me. But I didn't want to seem desperate. After hovering over the little green phone emblem with my thumb for at least a full minute, I finally pressed it. I put it on speaker as it began to ring. I halfway hoped it would go to voicemail.

"Hey Tess," Vito's voice came through the phone. He picked up on the third ring.

Damn.

"Vito, hey, how are you?"

"Feeling better, thanks," he responded. "I'm glad you got back to me. Do you remember my friend Katrina Lucas? I went to school with her."

"Yeah, I remember her. She came by the restaurant quite a bit when we were first getting going."

"She always thought a lot of you, so I called her after everything that went down here," he said. "She's been working for Francesco Fiorelli and helping him open his Frankie's restaurants in big cities all over the country. She's made quite a name for herself."

"Wow, that's amazing. He's all over the Food Network. I watch his shows all the time."

"Well, she's in Manhattan and working on getting a Frankie's open there next month. There's a job for you there if you want it. She said she would love to have you. She said for you to give her a call to talk about it as soon as possible."

The excitement in Vito's voice was palpable. He wanted this for me. I knew it wasn't just so he could make himself feel better about having to let me go. He's always encouraged me and really was a great boss. The restaurant industry was a brutal business but working for him and with the people at The Olive Branch made it fun. It was hard to imagine going somewhere else. Especially a high-end chain like Frankie's. But this was a big-time opportunity.

"Thanks Vito, that's amazing. I really don't know what to say." I stammered a bit.

"I just texted you her contact info." My phone dinged confirming I got the text. "You need to call her Tess. This will open so many doors for you."

"I know and I appreciate that. It's just I'm back home right now. A friend of mine growing up passed away," I said. "My best friend actually."

"Oh no, Tess, I'm so sorry," he said. He hesitated like he was going to say something more.

"What?" I asked.

"It's nothing. I guess I'm just a little surprised. I've never heard you talk about your family or friends growing up and I've known you for years."

"Yeah, I know," I said quietly. "I messed up some things when I was younger. Now I'm back home. I don't think I can just pick up and leave right away."

"I get that but you really need to at least call Katrina and explain the situation. You don't want to miss out on this," Vito said.

"I know, I'll call her," I responded. I blew out a silent breath and banged my head against the car seat. "I've got to go but thank you for everything. I do appreciate you talking to her and putting my name out there."

"Of course, don't mention it. Call me and let me know how it goes and if you are, okay. Don't lose touch," he said.

"I won't, I promise. Later."

This was so unexpected I didn't know what to think. On one hand, I couldn't help but be excited and terrified at the thought of working for a big restaurant in Manhattan. On the other hand, I just got home. Even after Tess's memorial, the Shays would need a lot of support. And my brother was starting his own business and could use some help. Could I really pick up and leave again only days after getting back?

--- --- --- --- --- --- --- --- ---

On the way home, I picked up some steak and cheese subs and fries. Healthy would not cut it tonight, I wanted comfort food. When we were younger, Benny and Jack could eat steak and cheese morning, noon, and night and be happy. I seriously doubted that had changed in the years I'd been gone. As I pulled up the drive, I saw Jack's truck already parked next to Benny's Jeep.

I tried to remember the last time people were waiting for me to come home. I shook that somewhat sad thought off, grabbed the sandwiches, and headed into the house.

I could hear Benny and Jack in the kitchen at the back of the house as I came through the door. When I got there, they were sitting at the little round kitchen table that we all used to drink juice and eat a snack at as kids. I guess things can come full circle. Only now they were drinking beer.

"Hey, I hope steak and cheese sounds good," I said as I came into the kitchen and dropped the greasy bags onto the table.

"When does steak and cheese ever not sound good?" Benny said while taking the sandwich I held out to him. Jack must have agreed wholeheartedly as he went after his own sandwich like a man who was starving. I grabbed some paper towels and sat down with the guys to eat.

"How are the Shays?" Benny asked. "I haven't been over to visit them yet."

I thought for a minute while I chewed my bite of sandwich. When I finally got it down, all I could come up with is one word.

"Lost. They are lost. I don't think they know how they are supposed to live without her. Leigh's Aunt Trudy is handling the funeral arrangements. They haven't been able to handle any of the details, except for saying they want me to do the eulogy."

The table got quiet. I tried eating a fry but my appetite had left so I swirled it around in my ketchup instead and hoped no one noticed if I didn't finish my food.

"I pushed her away." The words popped out unbidden. I had been thinking them but really had no intention of saying them out loud. "She wouldn't give up, though. She wouldn't let me shut her out."

I stared at the streaks of ketchup I had created on the foil sandwich wrapping and rubbed my grease and salt covered fingers together. I paper towel came into my field of vision. When I looked up, Jack was holding the paper towel roll and looking at me like he might want to beat me with it. I had pushed him away, too. A lot more harshly than I pushed Leigh. But he wasn't the type of person who could kick someone when they were down. He sighed and reached out to squeeze my hand in support.

"You remember the tractor incident?" Benny asked quietly.

I looked over at him. "You remember?" he asked again. "The tractor incident."

I choked out a laugh. "The incident that we swore eternal secrecy and to never speak of. No, don't remember it at all," I said with a sad smile.

"We were camping out at our farm," he started.

We all knew the story but maybe hearing Benny tell it would help. I didn't know how it would help. Maybe help ease the constant ache in my chest since hearing about Leigh's passing. Maybe help remind me that we had good times in our past, not just tragedy. Whatever it was, he seemed to think telling the story we all knew so well would help something. "You and Leigh were about 12 and Jack was 13. Mom didn't want you outside by yourselves in the tents, so she made me sleep out there with you. And it was hot as hell. I wanted nothing more than to go into the house with air conditioning and sleep in my bed. I was not happy with you guys at all."

"You were definitely grumpy," I said with a grin.

"Unlike the normal charming socialite that you usually are," Jack teased, cocking his beer bottle in Benny's direction. I couldn't help but chuckle.

Benny smiled. "If I remember right, you all were whining about it being hot too, but you didn't want to go inside because it was the last weekend to camp out before school started."

"It was Leigh that had the bright idea of taking your dad's tractor over to my parents' farm and getting in the pond," Jack said.

We all smiled. That night had been stifling hot and not a breeze to be found. Anyone with a lick of sense would've gone into the air-conditioned house and went to bed. Nope, not us.

"She had people so fooled. They all thought she was an innocent who would never cause trouble," I said.

"She at least used to think things through and have a plan." Benny paused and took a sip of his beer. "Except for that night."

We all laughed. Only kids could do something so stupid, live through it, and actually get away with it.

"I definitely thought we were done for when the cows followed us out the gate before we could get it closed," Jack said.

"The cows were no biggie, but I thought for sure we were busted when we got stuck in the creek," I added.

They both nodded in agreement.

"My God, we were so stupid," Benny said. "But stupidity can make for some great stories. I think it's time to share that story with all of Leigh's friends and family. Her life was cut short. And it is not fair. But they need to know that she had some great times and made the most of the time she had with her friends and family. That's what you need to make sure comes through in the eulogy."

I nodded. More stories swirled in my head. "I've got some ideas on how I'm going to put this together. Any pictures you have, please send them to me." They both nodded in agreement.

We made a half-hearted attempt to finish our sandwiches for a minute, but finally gave up. All of us were lost in our own memories of Leigh. I felt like there was a weight on my chest again. Like it was hard to breathe. It was a familiar feeling.

"I met with the bank today," Benny said. His statement snapped me out of my thoughts.

"How did it go?" I asked.

"Why?" Jack asked. He didn't mention that I told him already that Benny is taking over Uncle Rob's shop. It was Benny's news to tell. I appreciated Jack giving him the chance to tell it.

"Uncle Rob is retiring and I'm buying the shop from him," Benny said. "But I want to do some things, grow it, and make it my own. It takes money. More money than what the shop is worth right now. I met with a loan guy who specializes in small business loans and he was letting me know what I have to do. He said I may need collateral or a partner to co-sign or both. And I need to write a business plan."

"Wow," Jack said. "That's pretty huge. Congrats, my man. I hope you can get it all worked out. Let me know if I can help, though I don't know the first thing about writing a business plan."

"I do," I chimed in. They both looked at me like I had two heads. "What? I took some business classes in college and it's one of the first things they had us do."

For a minute, there was silence. Benny and Jack gave each other a look, silently communicating what they were both thinking. They didn't have to say anything. They were wondering how long I would be here. My conversation with Vito and the job offer from Katrina rose to the forefront of my mind, and I knew their concerns were justified. But, even if I did have to leave soon after the memorial, it wouldn't be like when I left for school. I wouldn't be sneaking off like I did all those years ago.

After high school was finally over, I pushed everyone away and literally left in the middle of the night, abandoning everyone important to me. Honestly, at the time, I thought it would be best for everyone. Even now, I'm not sure I was wrong. I was horrible to anyone who was near me or tried to help me. I was alienating everyone; the worst probably being Jack.

The last straw had been his senior prom.

"We don't have to go to the prom if you don't feel like it, Tessie," Jack had said to me as we were driving to the Crossroads Hotel, the one and only hotel in Crossroads, where the dance was being held. We were meeting up with Leigh and her boyfriend and a few other people there.

"I bought the stupid dress and got ready. We might as well go," I snapped. We spent the rest of the ride in silence. Jack drove, and I stared out the passenger window. I was so angry. All the time, I was angry. I just wanted people to leave me alone.

When we got to the hotel, our friends were waiting for us in the lobby, and we went into the ballroom together. Leigh put her arm through mine.

"How are you doing?" she asked.

"I'm fine," I said shortly.

"We're going to have so much fun tonight." She had a big smile, like she could be happy enough for both of us. I didn't respond to her enthusiasm.

We found a table, and the guys went to get us some punch, joking about if anybody had added anything special to it for the occasion. I sat at the table and listened to Leigh talk with some of the other girls.

"I love your dress, Tess! Where did you get it?" Mary, another girl at our table, asked. I shrugged my shoulders and watched the band. "I guess Benny picked it up at some place in the mall."

"Your brother picked your prom dress?" she asked incredulously. As I had just told her this, I didn't feel the need to answer again. Prom was not high on my list of things I cared about anymore. Though, to be fair to Mary, going to prom with Jack would've have meant everything in the world to me six months ago. Before. Before my parents died. Before we lost the only home I had ever known. Before my whole world fell apart. All that kept going through my head is that my mom should've been helping me get ready tonight. My dad should've been talking to Jack on the front porch and telling him to drive safe. Not Benny.

"I went with him to help pick something out," Leigh told Mary.

The guys came back with the punch and joined us at the table. Jack sat next to me and tried to put his arm around my shoulders. Instead of letting him, I got up and went to the bathroom without saying a word to anyone. I didn't need to go, but I wanted to be away from all of them. After wandering past the bathroom, I walked around the hotel a bit. I don't know how long I was gone, but when I got back, Jack was sitting at the table alone. I saw the rest of the group scattered around the dance floor.

"Hey, you feeling okay?" he asked. "You've been gone awhile."

I sat down next to him with a loud sigh. My entire demeanor screamed that I would rather be in any other place in the world than where I was. This whole prom thing seemed silly and superficial now. Who cares about dresses and hair and dancing.

"For the millionth time, I'm fine," I replied.

Jack was a great guy. He was funny, patient, kind, but even he had his limits.

He said nothing. After a few minutes, I stopped staring sullenly at the people dancing and looked over at him. He was looking at me with such a sad look on his face. I knew I was hurting him and everyone else around me, but I just didn't care. It was like something in me was broken. The part that used to care about my life and the people in it just stopped working.

Jack picked up his truck keys and stood up. "Come on."

"What are you doing?" I asked.

"Taking you home. You very clearly do not want to be here," he said as he turned to walk toward the exit.

He was right. I didn't want to be there. But I didn't want to be at home either. I really didn't know where I wanted to be.

I caught up to him and grabbed his arm to get him to stop walking away. "Jack, I didn't say we had to leave." I knew people were staring. Teenagers can smell impending drama from a mile away.

Jack turned to me and his face was so resigned, it made me take a step back in shock. It cut through all the anger I was constantly feeling and allowed me to feel something else. Shame for the way I was acting. It wasn't me. I kept hurting everyone around me. Lashing out at anyone who tried to get too close. I was in a sea of misery and the only way I could handle it was to spread it around apparently. For an instant, Jack cut through it all and reached the real me. But, it didn't last. The anger and pain rushed back over me and blocked off any other feelings.

"Tessie, I don't want to do this here. Please, let's leave, and we can talk somewhere private," Jack whispered.

"No, you have something to say, then say it!" I screamed.

Now, everyone at the prom was staring at us. I even heard the band falter, like they weren't sure if they should keep playing. One of my favorite teachers, Mrs. Peacock, had made her way through the crowd to me. She had grown up with my mom and knew me since the day I was born.

She came over and put her arm around me. "Tess let's go outside and get some air, honey. You need to calm down."

Stepping away from her and turning on Jack, I yelled, "I don't want to go outside and calm down. I want to know what your problem is."

Jack had been nothing but patient and kind with me since my parents had died. Perversely, the nicer he was to me, the meaner I got. It was like I was trying to push his buttons. I wanted a knock down, blow out fight. If nothing else, maybe it would get some of the anger out. But that wasn't Jack. He was the silent, angry type. He didn't do screaming matches.

So, I knew he was done when he yelled back at me. "My problem is you!" The rest of the room got silent. The band even gave up on playing. Why would they? No one was listening.

Jack ran his hands through his hair. "I can't do this anymore Tess!" he yelled. He pulled his tie loose and undid the first button of his shirt like it was strangling him.

I knew what was coming. And that I couldn't stop it.

"I know you have had a rough year," Jack said, no longer yelling. "The roughest. No one should have to go through what you and Benny have had to handle. I have done everything I can to help you deal with it. I know losing your parents like you did is not something you just get over. But you have to learn to live with it, Tess. They wouldn't want you to stop living, stop hanging out with your friends, and they definitely wouldn't want you to stop being a decent human being."

He turned away from me for a minute and took a deep breath, like he was trying to get control of his emotions. When he turned back towards me, I could see it on his face. We were over.

He sighed. "I hope you can be happy again. I know you will never be the same as before your parents died, but I hope you at least remember some of that girl and can bring her back. She's the girl I grew up with and fell in love with. But, I can't do this anymore, trying to make it work with this angry shell of a person you are now. You need help, Tess. You need to talk to someone - a professional - and get some help. But, you have to want to do it. No one can do it for you."

I stood in silence. I had nothing to say. It was like I was dead inside. I knew I should feel something, but I was numb.

"Would you take her home?" Jack asked Mrs. Peacock.

"Yes. Tess, I will be right back. I've got to go grab my purse," she said as she made her way through the crowd.

Jack looked at me one last time, then he turned around and left.

After he graduated high school, he immediately started working at his family's farm and taking classes part time at the community college. I still had one more year of school, but after the scene at prom, everyone left me alone. Which is what I wanted. I didn't go out on the weekends, get a part-time job, or even go to my own senior prom. I went to school and came home. Only to get Benny off my back and because I knew it would be a way out of this town, I applied to colleges. Luckily, my parents had college funds for both of us. Since Benny didn't go to college, he let me use the money they saved for him as well as my own, even though he probably could've used it trying to support us both.

I don't think I ever told him how much I really appreciated every-thing he did to keep us together and to take care of me. I just counted down the days until I could leave. The day I left for college, I got up hours before the sun was up, got in my car and drove away without saying anything to anyone. I left Benny and everyone else behind.

And now, I was back and asking the people I had hurt so much to trust that I wouldn't do it again. Jack and Benny were both looking at me like they were waiting for me to get up and bolt out the door any second. Pack my crap in my car and leave like I did all those years ago after high school. And, more recently, like I did last night when I packed up my life in northern Virginia and came home.

"I'm not leaving like that again." I looked both of them in the eye.

"Tess, you have a college degree and your whole life ahead of you," Benny said. "You could go anywhere in the world."

Images of New York City flashed in my head. The job that anyone in the restaurant business would give their favorite chef's knife for was mine if I wanted it. I should be thrilled. But, so far, excitement wasn't on the menu. All I felt was apprehension and guilt whenever I thought of the job that Vito had managed to get lined up for me. The offer had a time limit. Accepting it would mean leaving again and very soon. And the job would keep me away. There wouldn't be a lot of free time available to come all the way back home to Virginia for family visits. There wouldn't be time for me to make amends. To try to set things right.

I decided not to bring up New York. Not yet.

"I know that, but right now, I want to be here. It may not be forever. Who knows what will happen down the road, but I've grown up. I'm not a stupid, angry teenager anymore. Let me help you with this. Please. I owe you."

Benny looked at me in bewilderment. "You don't owe me Tess. What could you owe me?" he said a little angrily. "They were my parents too. I wanted to do right by them and you. They wouldn't have wanted us to be apart."

"I know," I said quickly. "I didn't mean it to sound like ... that." I didn't know what I was trying to say. I just knew I had deeply insulted my brother. "I'm sorry."

Benny stood up from the table and walked a few steps away. He had his back to Jack and me. He stood there for a minute, gathering his thoughts. I tried to catch Jack's eyes but he was very focused on staring at his now very cold fries.

Finally, Benny turned around an faced me. "You don't owe me anything. And you don't have any making up to do with me," Benny said. He sat back down at the table and looked me in the eyes. "We're good. We always were. I'm glad you're here for however long that ends up being."

I smiled at him. "Even if I move away at some point down the road, I promise it won't be like it was before. I won't be running away."

Throughout this exchange, Jack sat quietly, sipped his beer, and continued to stare at what was left of his food. He stood up after I finished speaking and threw his beer in the recycling and food wrappers in the trash.

"I'm going to head out. I have to get up early tomorrow. We have to do some bush hoggin in the fields." He said this while looking at Benny. He finally looked over at me. "I'll send some pictures for the memorial."

"Okay," I said. He turned to walk away but then turned back and looked at me. "Your field is still there. It's still clear. I'll see you around Tessie."

"Bye," I replied softly, but he was already going out the door. My field. The Hallowell Farm had a field that I used to run in every morning before school. The whole family started referring to it as "my field" and they always tried to keep it clear of brush for me.

Jack hadn't let go of the past, but maybe he left the door cracked for moving forward from here. Could we restore a semblance of what we once had? Not dating but being the friends we had once been. We were friends for far longer than we were lovers. Could I get that back?

It was something to hope for.

# Chapter 7

# BLAST FROM THE PAST

*"He must have known I'd want to leave you."*
*"No, he must have known you would always want to come back."*
— J.K. Rowling, Harry Potter and the Deathly Hallows

"What?" I groaned as my brother's knocking on the door woke me out of a deep sleep. I snaked my hand out from under the covers into the cold room just enough to reach my phone on the nightstand - 5:02. Rolling my eyes, I covered my head with the comforter. He's up and leaving for work at five in the morning. Some things don't change.

"I'm taking your car to the shop today. I'll leave you the keys to my Jeep. See you tonight," he called as he was going back down the stairs and conveniently giving me no time to argue.

I pulled the covers down and stared at the ceiling. My car would come home tonight with new tires, an oil change, and probably a long overdue tune-up. All of which would cost Benny, Uncle Rob, and the shop money. And they won't let me pay for a cent.

But they will let me write a business plan for them. I started thinking about the money I had saved and how I could use it to help Benny with the shop... if he would let me.

Laying in bed and staring at the ceiling, I thought of the business plan and how I would organize it. Then I started thinking about Leigh's eulogy, which I still needed to write. The next time I looked at the time, it said 5:48. Groaning, I swung my legs over the side of the bed and stood. Going back to sleep clearly would not happen. That's when my gaze landed on my old running shoes.

Over the years, I tried to get back into running the way I was before my parents died, but I just couldn't find the passion for it anymore after they were gone. My mom got me into running. When I was a little girl, I wanted to be with her all the time. When she went for a run, I begged her to take me with her. So, she started training me and teaching me to build up my endurance and go faster and farther. We would explore different paths and trails. Eventually, I would run more and more without her, but we would still go together at least once or twice a week.

With the memories of running with my mother going through my head, I went outside and climbed into Benny's Jeep. The Hallowell's field that I used to run in nearly every morning before school was a few minutes down the road. Leaving the Jeep parked at the gate, I climbed over the fence and hopped down into the field. I started walking the perimeter, trying to warm up and get a feel for the shoes again. After a few minutes, I broke into a slow jog. It didn't take long for my legs to remind me it had been some time since I tried to go for a run. My breath started coming a little harder and I could feel the exertion in my chest. I kept going, picking up my pace here, slowing down there until I made a couple of laps around the field. I stopped back at the gate where I parked the Jeep. The sun was beaming down at me, bright in the blue sky. It must be around seven now. A cool breeze blew across my face and birds chirped in the trees that dotted the field. It was peaceful. A calm I hadn't felt in a long time settled inside me. For a minute, I let my mind go quiet. And that's when I felt it. Being here felt right.

But, then my brain kicked back into gear and I remembered that I needed to call Katrina today about the job offer at Frankie's. I would be lying if I didn't say a little thrill of excitement ran through me at the thought of moving to New York and helping to get a new Frankie's restaurant established in Manhattan.

And then I thought of Benny and helping him get his dream off the ground. I wanted to be a part of it. I wanted to watch Benny grow Uncle Rob's garage into what he wanted. I wanted to see it happen. I wouldn't be able to from New York.

After my run, I came home and got cleaned up. Breakfast ended up being toast with what little butter I could scrape out of the bottom of the container. Benny needed some food in the house. The refrigerator was pathetically bare.

Deciding to stop by the Shays first and see if they needed anything from the store, I headed to their house. When I got there, the door was open with just the screen door shut. I knocked lightly and waved as I saw Mrs. Shay walking toward the door.

"Tess, hey, come on in." There was a little more warmth and feeling in her voice than she could manage yesterday. Though sadness and grief still shone in her eyes and coated her face, she had showered and put on fresh clothes, so I took that as a good sign.

"Hi Mrs. Shay." I gave her a hug. I didn't ask how she was doing or if she was okay. I remember after my parents died, everyone wanted to know if I was okay. What are you supposed to say? The truth? Most people wouldn't know what to do if you told them the truth. But, saying "I'm fine" to everyone you run into gets old quick. Of course, if I had taken the time to reach out to one of those well-meaning people, maybe I wouldn't have blown up every important relationship I had with my family and lifelong friends and snuck out of town in the middle of the night. But that was for contemplating on a different day.

We walked into the kitchen where Mr. Shay was drinking a cup of coffee and trying to eat some toast and scrambled eggs. He had showered too and was attempting to appear okay. I sat down at the table with them, being careful not to sit in the chair Leigh always used and accepted a cup of coffee from Mrs. Shay.

"I'm going to the store; Benny has no food in the house. I wanted to see if you need anything?"

Mrs. Shay looked around and shrugged. "I don't think so. People have been bringing so much food that I can't imagine we will eat it all."

"That's nice of everyone," I said.

She just nodded.

For a few minutes, we sat there, sipping our coffee, each lost in our thoughts. It was actually a little comforting and, hopefully; they got some comfort from sitting with me. There was no explanation or empty gestures required. We shared our grief in silence.

I finished my coffee and took a quick look through the refrigerator and cabinets to see if there was anything I could pick up for them. They needed milk and probably some more coffee and drinks for all the friends and family coming by. I added some things to my list and promised to be back in an hour or two.

I was making my way through Walmart, grocery list in hand, when I heard "Tess!" yelled from halfway across the store. Turning around, I saw Ruby Kemper, one of my mom's best friends. Ruby wasn't a small woman and if you didn't see her, believe me, you heard her. Because she wasn't a quiet woman either. She dressed loud, talked loud, and was always in everyone's business and lives. But she didn't have a mean bone in her body, and everyone loved her. She came rushing through the store, arms wide open to envelop me.

"Tessie, I can't believe it's you!" she yelled as she folded me into a big hug.

Hugging her back, I felt the sudden urge to cry. Why had I pushed this woman away too? I hugged her until I got some control over my emotions.

"Hey Ms. Ruby, it is so great to see you!" The words "you look great" were forming in my mouth, but died before I could get them out. One look and I realized this was not the Ruby Kemper I remembered.

"It's great to see you, too. I missed you so much! Your Uncle Rob told me you moved back home when I saw him yesterday. I can't wait to get together and catch up. I'm so glad you're back..., but I hate what brought you home," she finished quietly, the momentary happiness draining out of her face.

Ruby watched Leigh grow up right alongside of me. Leigh and I spent many Sundays after church at Ruby's, hanging out and talking about boys or clothes or movies, baking brownies or cookies, and laughing. Always laughing.

"Oh, honey," Ruby said, wrapping her arms around me. She said nothing else. She just stood there holding me in the middle of Walmart as the shoppers passed by around us. After a minute, I pulled back and really looked at her.

She looked much older than I remembered. Instead of her usually immaculate and colorful clothes, she wore a dull, well-worn sweat-shirt and faded jeans. She had no make-up on and her hair was flat and pulled into a ponytail, which just highlighted her streaks of gray. When I left town, this woman wouldn't have gone to 7-11 with a gray hair showing. Ruby never missed a hair appointment. She certainly wouldn't come to Walmart dressed like this, knowing she was bound to run into at least ten people she knew before she got past the produce.

What had happened to Ruby while I was gone? It couldn't all be because of the grief of Leigh's death. It was obvious this had been going on far longer than a couple of days.

"Do you want to come over tonight and have dinner with Benny and me? I'm trying to stock up the house now. I think he hasn't been home much lately, so there is no food. I was glad he at least had coffee."

She thought about it for a minute, but then I saw a little of the old Ruby come back and she gave me a big smile.

"Honey, I would love that. What do you want me to bring? Maybe some brownies?" She gave me a knowing look. Brownies were a weakness. There wasn't much I wouldn't do for a brownie and Ms. Ruby made the best homemade brownies, never box or store bought.

"Ummm, yeah," I said in my best five-year-old, like duh, voice.

Ruby laughed, and it was like some years and worry melted off her face. How long had it been since she laughed?

"What time?" she asked.

"How about seven? I know it's a little late, but I think Benny has been spending long hours at work and I have some more errands to run after getting the groceries home."

"Seven is perfect." She glanced into her cart. "And I better get going before my ice cream melts in a puddle on the floor."

Despite her melting ice cream, she wrapped her arms around me again and held me for another minute. She pulled back and studied my face like she was afraid I would disappear on her again.

"I'll be there," I whispered.

She nodded, "Leigh always knew you would find your way back to us, eventually. Benny and I started to lose hope over the years, but Leigh never did. She never gave up."

With that, she turned away and made her way toward the checkout area. Facing head on all the pain I had caused and hearing how the people I cared most about in the world tried to hold on to the hope that I would come back to them, was humbling. Knowing that I was too late coming back to the best friend anyone could ask for left me gutted. I would never have the chance to make things right with Leigh.

Shoppers bustled by, talking, laughing, arguing, but I was rooted to that spot. Carts clattered along the hard floor. It all faded into the background. My mind had left and traveled back to the past.

"Honey, why don't I drive you to college instead of Benny? We can see if Leigh can go, and she and I can get a hotel room and help you get set up in your dorm room, then scope out the town. I've never been to Blacksburg before. Maybe we can even go into Roanoke for a little shopping," Ruby said while she helped me fold my laundry to pack for school.

"Maybe," I uttered with a shrug, but that was the last thing I wanted.

It was the end of summer. I had graduated high school in May and now it was August. I was leaving to go to Virginia Tech the next day. Benny was going to follow me down and help me move into my dorm room. As the time for me to leave got closer, Ruby, Leigh, and even Uncle Rob started coming around more, no longer giving me the space they had been my whole senior year. They were trying to help me get ready to go and make sure I knew I could always come home and they would miss me.

It was suffocating.

The only thing that kept me going was knowing that I would be out of this place and away from them all soon. Away from the questions of how I was doing and did I need anything or worse, the advice on how to move on and suggestions to "talk to somebody." Logically, I knew it had been well over year, nearly two years in fact, since my parents died, but somehow, it still felt so fresh. Like it had just happened yesterday.

"I'll call over to Leigh's and see if she can go," Ruby was going on excitedly. "We'll get up bright and early so we can try to get there before most of the other freshmen."

I nodded but was cringing inside. Ruby was chattering on excitedly about going out to breakfast on the way down and shopping in Roanoke. Somewhere in the back of my mind, I knew I should be excited, too. But all I could think was this was something my mom would've loved. And, as hard as she tried, Ruby was not my mom and never would be.

When she finally left, I'd sat on the end of my bed in the waning light of evening. Benny would be home from work soon. He wanted to take me out to dinner, just me and him. I had no interest in going or even changing out of my torn jeans and worn-out sweatshirt. All of my packed suitcases and bags sat by the door waiting to be put into the car. So close to gone. I could just throw my bags in the car and leave now.

As soon as the thought occurred to me, it felt like a weight had lifted off my shoulders. There would be no goodbyes and we'll miss you's. I could just drive away. The dorms didn't open until around 9am but I could park outside and nap in the car while I waited if I had to. I just needed out of here. Before I had a chance to rethink or second guess, I started grabbing bags and throwing them in the car. I recognized this was crazy on some level, but the need to be away and start over fresh where no one knew me overpowered it.

As I was taking the last of my stuff to the car, I had thought of Benny coming home, looking forward to going to dinner, probably starving because he wouldn't want to ruin his appetite with lunch. Instead of me waiting for him, it would be an empty house. Groaning, I had closed the car door and went back inside. Going to dinner with my brother was the least I could do after everything he had done for me.

Later that night, after Benny and I had our dinner out and he went to sleep and hours before Ruby and Leigh came over, I wrote a note to Benny, ignoring the feelings of guilt and shame that crept into my psyche.

*Decided to beat the traffic. Don't worry about helping me move in. I only have a few bags of clothes, I'll manage. Tell Ruby I'm sorry, but maybe another time.*

*Love you,*

*Tess*

I stuck the note on the front of the fridge using the magnet we got from the aquarium on our last family vacation to Myrtle Beach. My mom had loved magnets and always got some as souvenirs when we went on family trips. My finger traced over this one, a family photo of us standing in front of fake palm trees and a beach backdrop in a magnet frame. I fought the sudden tears that came to my eyes. This was why I needed to leave. I couldn't get past anything surrounded by everyone and everything that reminded me of what had been lost. Taking one last look around at the house my brother tried so hard to make a home, I dimmed the kitchen light and left. A moment later, I started my car and headed down the driveway and away from this place. I had no intention of ever coming back.

"Sorry," someone muttered when they bumped me on their way down the aisle. My mind came back to the present where I was still standing in the middle of Walmart. Giving myself a mental kick, I went back to my list and tried to shake off the memories.

# Chapter 8

# DON'T YOU FORGET ABOUT ME

*"I hope you realize that every day is a fresh start for you. That every sunrise is a new chapter in your life waiting to be written."*

— Juansen Dizon, Confessions of a Wallflower

"Tess?" I heard Ruby call as she opened the front door after a light knock.

I tucked the eulogy for Leigh's funeral away under my pillow to work on more later and went downstairs. Ruby was already in the kitchen putting a plate of brownies on the counter. She hadn't changed from what she was wearing when I saw her earlier at Walmart. Ruby was always larger than life but not in a way that put people off. It was in a way that would bring people in and make them feel included. But something happened. She was different. Not just how she looked but she wasn't acting like the Ruby that I always knew. The Ruby I never expected to change. What had happened?

"Those brownies look amazing," I said as I gave her a hug. I felt her arms wrap around me and some of the tension eased. At least one thing hadn't changed. Ruby always gave the best hugs.

"Can I get you a glass of wine?" I asked as she took a seat at the little kitchen table.

"Sure, sounds good," she replied while looking around. "I haven't been here in a long time."

"Do you get to see Benny much?" I asked.

"Not really. He spends most of his time working. And, I've been... busy."

I sat the glass down in front of her and waited for her to elaborate, but she just sat there.

"Ruby, what happened to you? You are not the same woman I grew up with," I said with a little exasperation.

She said nothing for so long; I wondered if she was going to respond at all.

"Why did you leave like you did?" she asked.

My breath caught, and the blood drained from my face to go hide somewhere down around my feet. I was caught off guard though I should have expected this conversation was going to happen. I wasn't expecting it right this minute.

Ruby sat quietly, waiting for me to respond.

I got up and checked the lasagna in the oven. When I turned back around, Ruby was staring at me. Still silent. Still waiting.

"I needed to get away," I mumbled.

"And you thought leaving with no one knowing, without saying goodbye, or thank you, was the best way?" Ruby asked pointedly.

"No," I said, staring at the floor. I couldn't bring myself to look at her.

"It devastated your brother," she said.

That was a kick to the gut. I turned away from Ruby and looked out the kitchen window over the sink. I guess I knew that I was hurting Benny, but I tried to tell myself that it was for the best. His life would be better if he didn't have to deal with me.

"Do you know how much he gave up for you, Tess?" Ruby sighed. "They were his parents, too. And, on top of losing them, he had to give up his life to take care of his baby sister. And he did it with no complaints. Or regrets, as far as I know. Then, he lost you too."

I slumped a little at the sink. Having it said out loud how much I hurt my brother made it much harder to rationalize it to myself. Saying 'I didn't mean to hurt him' sounded lame and childish. Saying 'I'm sorry' wasn't enough. Did I wish I would've handled some things differently? Better? Yes. Still, I wouldn't have changed leaving. I can't explain the desperation that drove me to leave. If I would've stayed... I don't know what would've happened. Knowing the place I was in, it wouldn't have been good. And maybe the outcome would've been more devastating for Benny if I had stayed than it was because I left.

Turning back towards Ruby, I opened my mouth to try to explain it and get her to understand. But the words wouldn't come. Maybe I still wasn't ready to share how dark a place I was in all those years ago. I'm doing better than I was then but I will never be the Tess everyone remembers from before my parents died. If I was being honest with myself, even today, part of me wanted to get in my car and drive to New York and never look back.

I sat down at the table. I said nothing, so Ruby just put one of her hands over mine and sipped her wine with the other. We could hear the tick, tick, tick of my mom's old chicken shaped timer on the counter making sure the lasagna didn't burn; otherwise, the kitchen was silent.

I was rubbing a groove in the table with my finger and thinking about how much this simple wooden kitchen table was a part of the background of so many of my memories. "God, this table has seen a lot," I said quietly, briefly breaking the silence.

Eight years ago, it was Benny sitting next to me at this table our first night in this house. He had his hands wrapped around a cup of coffee. It was in Dad's favorite mug. Ruby just left to drop Leigh and Jack off at home, and my brother's three best friends were picking up the last load of things from our old house. My parents had taken out a second mortgage to fix up some things on the farm just before they died. The small life insurance plans they had couldn't pay it off and the money would quickly run out trying to make the payments. Benny didn't make enough to pay for everything, so the bank foreclosed.

"I'm sorry we lost the farm," Benny said.

I shrugged my shoulders. "Not your fault."

I didn't care about losing the farm. I didn't care that the house he got for us to live in was old and rundown. I didn't care that it was drafty in my new room and definitely had mice. I did not care.

But I couldn't tell him that. I couldn't tell him I just didn't care about any of it.

"I know this place doesn't look like much right now, but I will fix it up. May have to do it a little at a time, but it will look better," Benny said while looking around the old kitchen. I knew he was mentally making a list of things that needed to be done. In the back of my mind, I knew I should do the same so I could help him. But wanting to improve something would mean I had to care about it in the first place.

"Did you and Ruby get your room setup?" Benny asked.

I stared at the old table. I could feel his eyes on me. He was working hard to make things better for me. To make me happy. But the best I could do for him was to keep my mouth shut. I was scared of what would come out if I opened it. It wouldn't be talking. It would be screaming. Screaming for him to back off, for Ruby to go home, for everyone to just leave me alone. The best thing I could do for everyone around me was to not say anything.

So, I just nodded.

The chicken timer went off, snapping me back to this moment here with Ruby. I pulled the lasagna out of the oven and put in a

French loaf I picked up at the store to get warm and brown. Ruby sat silently watching me pull dishes down and get the butter out of the refrigerator.

"Is Benny joining us?" she asked.

"No, I texted him earlier, and he said he was trying to get some stuff done at work and would be late."

When everything was ready, I put a plate of lasagna in front of Ruby and sat down next to her with my plate. We each stared at the food for a few minutes in silence. Each lost in our own thoughts. I had never felt awkward around this woman in my life. She was like a mother to me, even when my mom was alive.

"I'm sorry I hurt you, I hurt Benny and Leigh, I'm sorry, but I had to get away."

After a moment, Ruby patted my hand again. "I know, honey," she said. "I think we all knew, even then. Benny was upset. He worried about you, but I think he understood you needed to leave."

She leaned over and wrapped one arm around me, giving me a squeeze as she used to call it. I put my head on her shoulder. We stayed that way for a few minutes.

"We better eat before it gets cold," I said, straightening back up in my chair. Ruby picked up her fork and took a bite.

"This lasagna is good," Ruby said. "Really good. Where did you get the recipe?"

"Oh, I worked in an Italian restaurant for the past couple of years. Picked up some pointers from the owner, Vito. Even though I majored in restaurant and hospitality management, I also took some cooking classes and really liked it. I've been taking more classes on-line and watching a lot of Food Network."

"Well, if the lasagna is any indication, it's paying off," Ruby said.

"Thanks." I smiled. A small compliment from Ruby made me feel better than the highest praise from any of my cooking teachers over the years.

"So, what's been going on with you?" I asked quietly.

Ruby sighed. "I got sick a while back. Then I got better. Kind of..."

"A little vague Ruby."

She put her fork down on her plate and took a big sip of wine.

"I have MS. Multiple sclerosis," she said. "I was diagnosed about two years ago. I had been having pain and numbness in my legs off and on for about a year and then I would get so tired, and it would last for days. But I didn't go to the doctor until I started having trouble with my vision. I was seeing things in double or they would be blurry."

"Oh my goodness, Ruby." I scooted my chair closer to hers, put my arms around her, and laid my head on her shoulder. "I love you." It was all I could think to say.

She patted my arm, "I love you too, honey."

For a minute, we sat like this, holding each other.

"I've been working with doctors trying to find the right medication for me. It's been a long road, but I'm able to get out and about again. For a while, I was afraid to go anywhere. I didn't trust my eyes for driving. I had to go on disability. It started out as short term and then turned into long term. I had to give up my teaching position at the high school."

"You don't teach anymore?" I asked, shocked.

"Actually, I'm getting back to it. I've been picking up some substitute teaching jobs, and I'm looking for a permanent position for the next school year."

"That's great," I said. "I'm sorry I wasn't here to help you."

Ruby nodded. There wasn't anything else to say.

After dinner, Ruby and I took our wine and brownies to the living room and got comfortable on the old sofa. I turned on the television and flipped through channels when I came across The Breakfast Club. Emilio Estevez, Molly Ringwald and the rest of the Brat Pack were dancing around a smoke-filled high school library.

My breath caught in my throat as I watched. All night, it felt like something was missing. Someone was missing.

Leigh.

Leigh loved all the John Hughes movies. She could recite all of them line for line without missing a beat. It used to drive me crazy. I would constantly remind her that neither of us was even born when these movies were made.

"Don't I know it!," Leigh would reply, hanging her head in sadness. "I missed my decade, Tess. I'm a total 80s girl. It is so not fair. If I was born sooner, I could've met up with Judd Nelson somehow and he could've shocked the hell out of my parents showing up to take me out with an earring in his ear, hair sticking up all over the place, wearing clothes he probably picked up off the floor..."

I would then remind her that Judd Nelson was a middle-aged man by the time she was born, and God knows how old he was when she was old enough for him to date without going to prison for it. If Judd Nelson, or anyone that remotely looked like his character, Bender, from The Breakfast Club ever showed up for their daughter, Leigh's parents would've called the police so fast Judd wouldn't have got one high-top clad foot through the front door.

Ruby sat next to me on the sofa, and I saw a tear trail down her face. We said nothing. We drank our wine and ate our fair share of the brownies. Then we split the portion of brownies that Leigh would've eaten and ate that too while we watched Judd Nelson win over Molly Ringwald and walk off in the distance on a high school football field.

# Chapter 9

# MENDING FENCES

*"The scariest thing about distance is you don't know whether they'll miss you or forget about you."*
— Nicholas Sparks, The Notebook

After Ruby left, I went up to my room and pulled my journal out again to write some more passages for Leigh's eulogy. I talked about brownies, John Hughes movie nights, and Pepto Bismol pink bedrooms. I did my best to capture on paper who my friend was when we were growing up and how relentless she was in trying to keep us connected. I pushed her away time and time again. But she never gave up.

The words started to swim around the page as my eyes got heavy. It didn't take too long before I drifted off to sleep.

The sound of an engine was my alarm clock the next morning. Benny's Jeep was warming up outside. I didn't even hear him come in last night and he was already leaving this morning. Slowly cracking open my eyes, I could see the morning sunlight coming through my windows. It was 6:30. This was sleeping in to him. I rolled my eyes and groaned, then put my head under the pillow until I heard the tell-tale crunch of tires on gravel as Benny drove down our long driveway.

Rolling over and fluffing the pillows, I tried to curl up and go back to sleep but it was a lost cause. My mind was already awake and thinking about everything that had happened the past couple of days; all the people I had reconnected with and all the people I still had yet to see. With a sigh, I flung the covers back and got up in the cold room. The mornings were still chilly though soon enough the sweltering Virginia heat and humidity would blanket everything in its suffocating embrace. I tried to remember that while I cursed the cold air as I pulled clothes out and quickly dressed.

Running had felt good yesterday so I was going to start the day that way again. I put on my running shoes and pulled my top blanket up on my bed, covering the knotted-up sheets underneath. That was my version of making the bed. It drove Benny crazy. His bed was made with such precision, the strictest military drill sergeant would have been proud.

Within twenty minutes I was back at Jack's field parked outside the gate. My car had never looked or run so well. Uncle Rob and Benny had put new tires on it and gave it a much-needed tune up and probably new brakes. I needed to do something for them to say thank you. Plus, I hadn't seen Uncle Rob yet since I've been back. If I was being honest with myself, I had been avoiding him. I got nervous in the pit of my stomach every time I thought about going to see him; he would not let me off the hook as easily as Benny and Ruby had.

Uncle Rob had been there for us since we were born and did everything he could to support us after our parents died. The last conversation I had with him before I left hadn't gone well. He was the only person who called me on my bullshit attitude and didn't treat me with kid gloves.

"You know you aren't the only one around here that lost your parents," Uncle Rob yelled. I was sitting at the kitchen table in our house while Uncle Rob paced around the small room waiting on the coffee pot to finish its percolations. It was about 4 a.m. and Benny was on his way back home from being out looking for me. They'd both been looking since about two, when Benny realized my car wasn't in the driveway. Uncle Rob found me driving through downtown Harrisonburg. The streets had been empty, all the businesses closed, and the homes dark. The sound of a loud car horn had broken the silence. Looking in the rearview mirror, I saw my uncle's truck on my bumper. Not caring about the double lines, he pulled up beside me, rolled down his passenger window and pointed to the side of the road, yelling to me to pullover.

When I came to a stop on the side of the road, Uncle Rob came around to my driver's side window. "Tess, what are you thinking?" Not waiting on any type of response, he walked out in the middle of the empty street and started pacing. He looked like he was literally about to pull his hair out. After a couple of deep breaths, he stopped pointed at me. "Get your ass home or, so help me, that car of yours will be nothing more than a shitty lawn ornament by the time I'm done with it."

He followed me on my bumper the entire way home and started yelling as soon as we got in the house.

"You know your brother and me open the shop in less than three hours. People depend on us to be there. We have jobs scheduled that need to be completed so people can have their cars when they need them. That's part of being a responsible adult. You are not a kid anymore, Tess. You leave for college in two weeks. You need to grow up. Your brother had to grow up and take on huge responsibility and it's about time you did your fair share too."

My uncle had a point. I should feel bad because he and my brother would be exhausted today at work. I could already see the bags under my uncle's eyes. But, I didn't feel any guilt. I didn't feel anything except for maybe a little thankful that he would have to leave soon to get ready for work.

Remembering that last encounter with him got my heart racing faster than the light jog I was doing around the field warranted. I would have to face him. The longer I avoided him, the harder it was going to be. Uncle Rob was a good man, but he wasn't an easygoing man. He wasn't afraid to call people on being an asshole and he wouldn't just let it go if you hurt him or worse, someone he cared about. I didn't want our first encounter to be at Leigh's funeral.

With a sigh, my jog slowed to a walk. I would go to the shop today. It would take more than one visit and one conversation to get right with Uncle Rob again, but I needed to start somewhere. The business plan would be a good excuse because it was a valid one. Maybe it would give us something to focus on and discuss without getting into the past right away.

Even if Uncle Rob let me change the focus today, he wouldn't let the past go forever. He would want to hash it out and get some explanations. The problem is, I don't know if anything I said would be good enough. He cared for Benny and me like we were his own kids and when I left like I did, I know I hurt him worse than almost anyone ever had.

I was walking around the field, lost in thought, picking at some stray long grass along the border of the fence when I heard a truck door.

Jack's truck was parked next to my car and he was climbing over the fence. The sun was shining on him as he walked towards me, highlighting the blond in his light brown hair. He hadn't shaved and was showing at least two or three days of beard on his face. His wasn't a fashion statement like you see on movie stars or in magazines; spring was a busy time on the farm. He just hadn't had the time or energy to shave. On purpose or not, he did look good.

There were still traces of the boy I grew up with in his face, but he only showed up here and there in a grin or a quick laugh. Otherwise, the boy Jack was gone. He was a man now. You'd have to be dead or close to it not to notice that he carried himself like a man with strength and confidence.

"Hey, I was driving by and saw your car," he said as he got closer.

"Hey," I said as he started walking next to me. My mind was racing a little bit. It used to be perfectly natural for Jack to show up at the field when he knew I would be running, but we lost that comfortableness a long time ago. "Where are you headed?" I asked before things could get awkward.

"I'm going to get some feed for the horses and pick up some deworming meds for the cows. What are you up to today?"

"Ha, I was just thinking about that." I stopped walking and looked out over the field.

Jack leaned back against the fence, calm and relaxed, and waited on me to go on. I felt a tinge of jealousy that he knew what he was doing today, that he was sure about his relationships with his friends and family, that he knew who he was and his place in the world.

"Benny and Uncle Rob fixed up my car. I need to go by the shop and thank them and maybe get started on the business plan for Benny," I said after a minute. "I think Benny meets with the small business loan guy at the bank next week."

"Have you seen Rob since you've been back?" Jack asked.

"No." I couldn't hold back the long sigh that escaped.

Jack looked at me and his expression said it all. It was a mix of "I'm not sure that's a good idea" and "good luck with that".

"Thanks, I know how well this is going to go," I said with a little laugh.

Jack smiled. "He's your uncle and he loves you. You guys can work through this, it just may take some time."

We started walking again and headed back to the fence gate.

"So did you stop just to say hi?" I asked.

"No, my folks heard you're back," he said. "They asked about you and if I'd seen you."

The swarm of bees known as anxiety that seemed to have a permanent residence in my stomach perked up. Another person I wasn't sure I was ready to face was Jack's mom. Jenny Hallowell cared for me like I was one of her own and was thrilled when Jack and I started dating in high school. And then I broke his heart and humiliated him at his senior prom. Jesus may forgive but a mother doesn't forget. In a place where we all went to church together, school together, the same Walmart together, Mrs. Hallowell managed to avoid seeing or speaking to me after that night. I haven't seen her since she took our picture standing on the front porch before we left to go to the prom all those years ago.

"Oh." I grabbed another blade of long grass to have something to do with my hands. "How is everyone?"

"Doing good. TJ is taking over more and more of the business end of running the farm. Dad and Mom are actually travelling more and leaving the farm to us to take care of. We're expanding into the horse business now."

"TJ convinced your dad?" I remembered Mr. Hallowell had always been dead set against getting into the business of breeding, training, and selling horses. Said it was a money pit and quick way to end up bankrupt. He and TJ would argue about it all the time.

"Well, not quite. It was Max,'" he said.

"Max?"

"Yep," he sighed as we reached the gate where his truck and my car were parked.

We both climbed over the fence like we always did, instead of bothering with opening the gate. Jack opened the door to the cab of his truck and pulled out a thermos. Then he put the tailgate down to sit on and poured some coffee in the thermos lid. I sat beside him and drank some when he passed the lid to me.

"Max ran off about three years ago. Him and Dad had a big blow-up fight because Max wanted to try riding in the rodeo circuit."

"The rodeo?" I said with a little bit of disbelief.

"It has always been a dream of his. Not that he told any of us that. I knew he loved horses, loved riding but never imagined that's what he wanted to do. You wouldn't know it by the way he acts, but he's a very private person underneath it all."

Max Hallowell was always the life of the party type of guy. Friendly, cute, charming, and well-liked, he always had a joke ready to break the ice or lighten someone's mood. He was the guy you thought was going to have a blessed, easy-going type of life. He had the same pressures of working on the farm and keeping the family business going as everyone else in the Hallowell clan, but it never seemed to get to him. He rolled with the punches and never seemed to take anything seriously.

"I guess he decided one day that he was going to give it a shot. He told my parents he needed some time away from the farm and was going to South Dakota. He met some guys that were amateur riders and they got some jobs on a ranch out there. In exchange for work, they would get room and board and to train for rodeo competitions. He had already competed in some amateur competitions and didn't tell any of us."

"Holy crap. I don't think I ever, in a million years, would've imagined Max doing that," I said.

"It took us all by surprise. Mom was fit to be tied when he left. She had it in her head he was going to get himself killed. Dad wasn't much better. He told Mom "if the boy wants to get his head kicked in by a damn horse, who are we to stop him?" he said trying to mimic his father's deep, baritone voice. "It was not a good time in the Hallowell house."

"I can imagine," I said. "But, how does this tie into TJ convincing your dad to breed horses?"

"Well, things were tense for a long time around the house after Max left. He would call and let us know how he was doing. Eventually, Dad and Mom calmed down. It did not thrill them, but I think they were trying their best to live with it. Mom hung the schedule for his competitions on the refrigerator and we would all take turns leaving the farm to go see him and watch him compete. Things were alright for a while." Jack paused as he took a gulp of coffee from the thermos lid. "Then, he got hurt. He got hurt bad."

"He was competing in Arizona. None of us were able to make it to that one. He got thrown off the bronco and landed badly. He had a concussion, and he was kicked and trampled by the bronco before they could get it away from him. He had broken ribs and an arm, multiple contusions, and torn abdomen and groin muscles."

"Mom and Dad flew to Arizona to be with him in the hospital. TJ, Nick, and me had to stay behind and keep the farm going. Dad made a deal with Max in the hospital. Give up the rodeo and we would get into the horse business. Max could be up to his eyebrows in horses if that's what he wanted but no more rodeo."

"Wow, I guess I can see why he changed course if he thought it would help keep Max home and safe," I said. "Did it bother TJ at all, the way it came about?"

"No, Dad called TJ first before he talked to Max. Dad said Max was in rough shape and it would be a long recovery. He and Mom couldn't handle watching him go through recovery to turn around and go right back to the rodeo. He said Mom was ready to hog tie Max and lock him in the cellar if she had to. Dad thought getting into horses might be a more effective way to keep Max around. TJ was immediately on board and started looking into what they would need to do to get started."

"Your parents are pretty awesome."

"Yes, they are," he said, nodding his head. "Yours were too".

"I know."

He hopped off the tailgate. "And Benny's not half bad," he said with a smile.

I smiled back. "He's got some good points."

I handed the thermos lid to Jack and hopped down. He would need to get going. He'd probably already stayed longer than he planned. Jack closed up the tailgate and paused, resting his arms on the back of the truck. It seemed like he was trying to choose his next words. Finally, he turned around and looked at me.

"I missed you. I didn't realize it until I saw you sitting in your car in front of my house. But, I've missed you for years. How can you miss someone without knowing that you are missing them?" he said, more to himself than to me it seemed.

So many emotions swirled in me at that moment that it was hard to figure out what I was feeling. Happy that he had missed me, sad that we lost so many years, nervous about what happened next. It was hard to define.

"I missed you too Jack. For so long, I've missed you. I'm sorry I hurt you. I'm sorry for the way I handled things, the way I ended things, and the way I ran away and didn't look back."

Jack moved forward and wrapped his arms around me in a hug, and I laid my head on his chest.

"No more apologies, at least not to me," he replied. "I'm not sure where we go from here. I can't pretend to know all the answers. But one thing I do know is we have to put the past behind us. So, from this point forward, you've apologized for the past and I've forgiven you. It's done, as far as I'm concerned. And now, you and I can take it a day at a time and see where things go, good friends like we always were or possibly something more if that's what we both end up wanting."

"Does that sound good to you?" he asked, pulling away so he could look me in the eyes.

"Yes, it sounds perfect. I need to figure out some things for myself before trying to do anything more with us right now than rebuild our friendship," I said. After a moment's hesitation, I quietly added, "but, I like leaving the door open for something more."

"Me too," he said. He walked around and got into his truck and started it.

"You know my family is going to be at Leigh's funeral," he said. "Maybe you should come by the house and see them. It's going to be a hard enough day without the added stress of worrying about running into my mom."

And there go the bees again. The thought of facing Jack's mom was going to give me a panic attack.

"I don't think it's going to go as bad as what you've built it up to be in your head," Jack said. "Why don't you come over for dinner tonight?"

"But, Benny," I started but Jack cut me off.

"Bring Benny too. It might make it a bit more comfortable for you to have him there, and we always have more than enough food."

I grew up with Jack and have known his family almost as long as I've known my own. They were an extension of me. I knew coming back and making things right with the people that I pushed away the hardest would not be easy. But it was going to be worth it to get back what I had lost.

"Okay," I said after a moment. "I'm going to the shop later and I will see if Benny can come too. I'll text you and let you know."

"Sounds good. The dinner bell is at 8 p.m., as always," he said as he shifted the truck in reverse.

I nodded and stepped away as he backed the truck up and turned around. He waved and pulled out onto the road.

The sun was high in the blue sky as I got in my car and started it. The morning was already getting warmer, and I looked forward to the day despite my anxiety over trying to clear the air with Uncle Rob and the rest of the Hallowell's. This had been a long time coming and it felt like a weight was slowly lifting off my chest. I was finally facing everyone I cared about. They were going to be part of my life again. And maybe they were what I had been missing all these years.

The shadow that blanketed my happiness was that Leigh wasn't here to see it. I would never get the chance to make things right with her. But, the one thought that comforted me was that I really didn't need to. Leigh stuck by me with a relentlessness that bordered on obsession. She refused to be pushed away. She was the one person I kept the door cracked for over the years. Losing her left a hole in my life that will always be there, but I know I will live with it better by keeping the people I care about most in my life. So, with these thoughts going through my head, I headed home to start my day.

# Chapter 10

# OPEN DOORS

*"I wondered if that was how forgiveness budded; not with the fanfare of epiphany, but with pain gathering its things, packing up, and slipping away unannounced in the middle of the night."*

— Khaled Hosseini, The Kite Runner

I parked outside Uncle Rob's shop. It was only 9:30 but Benny and Uncle Rob had already been at work for hours at that point and would be ready for some coffee. I grabbed the drink holder that held three cups of steaming coffee firmly in place with a pile of creamers and headed inside.

When I stepped through the door, it was like going back in time. Everything was the same as I remembered it. A bell jingled as the door closed behind me. The competing scents of grease, coffee, and the lemon cleaner that Uncle Rob used to clean the waiting area assaulted me. The white tile floor had scuff marks in the same places, the service desk was still a bright shade of turquoise blue that Uncle Rob hated but never got around to changing, and an old couch with cracked vinyl cushions sat against one wall facing an old television hanging on the opposite wall.

"Be right there," my uncle yelled, his voice coming through the door behind the service desk that led to the garage. I glimpsed him standing next to a minivan he had up on the car lift. He looked a lot grayer than I remembered, but otherwise he hadn't changed. Never a big man, he was about a foot shorter than Benny and dressed in one of the collared, short-sleeve polo shirts that he bought for the shop, a pair of jeans, and work boots. Uncle Rob wore a version of this same outfit every day, working or not. The only thing that changed was the color of the polo shirt. I smiled. It was comforting to know that he hadn't changed.

He was talking to Benny, who was changing the van's tires. I couldn't hear what they were saying, but it seemed to be a happy, relaxed conversation. Uncle Rob patted Benny on the shoulder and headed my way. When he looked up and saw me, he stopped for a second and his expression almost brought me to tears. He went from surprised to happy to a mixture of angry and sad all in the blink of an eye.

I walked around the service desk and into the garage and set the coffees on the workbench that ran along the wall.

"Hi Uncle Rob," I said. He didn't answer. I tried to hold his gaze but couldn't. I looked behind him and saw Benny watching us. He gave me a smile and went back to working on the van.

Pulling my eyes back to my uncle, I fumbled for words. "I'm sorry. I know that doesn't fix anything, but I am sorry for how I behaved, for making you worry, and for running off like I did."

"You didn't just runaway Tess, you stayed away," he said.

"I know. But I'm back now. I won't run off like that ever again. Promise," I said firmly, looking him in the eyes. I needed him to know I meant it. The only problem was that even as I said the words, the job offer I still hadn't followed up on flashed through my head. The incredible offer that would take me far away from the people that I was becoming increasingly more desperate to reconnect with and have back in my life.

For what felt like an eternity, he stood there, and I began to wonder if he could read my mind. I wouldn't have been surprised. But then he closed the distance between us and pulled me in for a hug. I sighed with relief and a little more weight lifted off my chest. "I'm glad you're back."

"Me too," I said.

Benny walked over. "One of those coffees mine?"

"Yes, right, coffee," I said. I let Uncle Rob go and began passing out my coffee peace offerings.

"Uncle Rob, here's black with a little bit of cream. Benny, black with a little bit of sugar." I handed each of them their cup.

"And yours that is cream and sugar with a little bit of coffee," Benny joked.

"Ha ha." I rolled my eyes. "I actually take it the same as Uncle Rob now."

We grabbed some stools to sit on and it got quiet as we each enjoyed that first glorious sip. The first sip of coffee is always the best.

"You guys busy today?" I asked, trying to start the conversation.

"Yeah, we have a few jobs lined up," Uncle Rob responded. "We keep a pretty steady stream of work going most days."

"Benny said you are retiring?"

Uncle Rob shrugged. "Not entirely. I'll still be around to help Benny, but I don't want to run the place anymore. Time to let someone else take the reins." He clapped Benny on the shoulder. The pride he felt for my brother was clear. A tinge of jealousy washed over me, but I quickly dismissed it. I had no right to feel jealous. I used to be close to my uncle too and would be again. The door had opened. It would just take a little more time to get back to where we once were.

"We need to work on your business plan," I told Benny. "You meet with the small business guy at the bank next week."

Benny nodded. "I've been jotting down some ideas like you asked. I'll finish today and bring it home tonight."

"Benny's got high hopes for this place. I have to admit, I'm curious to see what he does with it," Uncle Rob said. "He got us into fixing up and customizing old cars after we close up for the day. He's been showing some at local shows and has even sold a few."

"Benny, that's great!" I was truly excited for my brother. This was something he loved to do. Benny and my dad kept our old truck running for years. It's not that we couldn't afford to get a new one; it was just something they enjoyed doing. Benny was always fixing up old tractors and lawn mowers for our friends and neighbors when we were growing up. He made some good money doing it.

"There is a salvage yard off Airport Road that's become Benny's favorite hangout. If he's not here or at home, you can find him there," Uncle Rob told me.

"Actually, that's part of the business plan," Benny said. "Bryan is looking to sell."

"You want to buy the salvage yard?" Uncle Rob asked with surprise.

Benny nodded. "Yep, I do," he said with assurance. "That's why I spend so much time there. I'm doing an inventory of everything Bry has and learning the business from him. It would tie in well with the plans I have for here."

Uncle Rob was quiet for a minute, like he was debating whether to say what was on his mind. He usually didn't hesitate too long before telling you what he thought.

"I'm glad you got plans Benny, and I'll do what I can to support you; but be careful you don't bite off more than you can chew."

"I won't," Benny said calmly.

Uncle Rob drank his coffee in an effort to stop himself from saying more, I thought. I sipped my coffee to hide my smile while I watched him wrestle with figuring out how much he should say. He usually wasn't so torn about whether to provide his opinion. I imagine he was worried about Benny getting in over his head, but he also wanted to be supportive and believe in him.

Fortunately, I knew a great way to change the subject and take some focus off Benny.

"Are you busy tonight?" I asked Benny.

"Not really. There isn't anything I have to get done tonight," he said. "Why? What's up?"

"Jack asked us to have dinner. At his house. With his family. That would include his mom." I suddenly became very interested in the coffee cup in my hand. I could only imagine what Uncle Rob and Benny were thinking. If Jack's mom was the Russian fighter, Ivan Drago, in Rocky IV, I was Apollo Creed. Doomed from the get-go.

"Dinner at the Hallowell's. It's been a while since we've done that," Benny said.

"Jack thought it would be a good idea before Leigh's funeral. Maybe clear the air. He thought I might be more comfortable if you're with me, so I have someone in my corner."

"The Mickey to your Rocky?" Uncle Rob joked, somehow reading my mind—again!-about how I was picturing this night would go.

"I don't think Jenny Hallowell is going to take a swing at me," I said dryly. Though, I couldn't entirely rule it out.

"Is Jack not in your corner?" Benny asked a little pointedly.

"He is," I said. "We met up this morning and talked. It was good. I think we put a lot of what happened before to bed. It's just that you know the whole family, too. You're friends with his brothers, and Mr. and Mrs. Hallowell love you. It might help relieve any tension there might be between me and them to have you there."

"Well, when you put it that way, it sounds like loads of fun," Benny said sarcastically. He got up from the stool and tossed his cup across the garage into the trash. "I should get back to work."

"Benny, please," I pleaded. I was not above begging at this point. I did not want to go to this dinner by myself.

Benny rubbed his hand over his head with a sigh. "Fine," he said with resignation. "Jack's right. It would be best to see them before you run into them at the funeral. That's going to be a hard enough day without adding that kind of drama."

"I know," I said, while standing up. The kidding around and happy feeling in the room vanished at the mention of Leigh's funeral. "I better get going. I'm going to stop in at the Shays again to check on them, and then work on the eulogy."

"Yeah, we better get back to work," Uncle Rob said, giving me another hug. "Don't worry about tonight. Jenny may have been upset about how things ended with you and Jack, but she also knows what you were going through then. I think she will be better than you think."

"Thanks, Uncle Rob. I hope you're right." When he tried to turn away, I held on just a little longer. I had missed him so much. He put his arms back around me and held me.

"Dinner at 8?" Benny asked.

"Always," I replied. I finally let Uncle Rob go as Benny went back to the van.

"We're good honey." Uncle Rob smiled.

I smiled back and nodded. "I'll see you later."

After leaving the garage, I racked my brain about what to do as I drove to the Shays house. I was beginning to feel more and more at home with each passing day. And, despite the grief I had over Leigh's death, a feeling of genuine happiness and comfort that I hadn't felt in a long time was starting to take residence inside me. I didn't want to lose it. But, this was a once in a lifetime opportunity that Vito got for me on a silver platter.

I sighed as I pulled to a stop in front of the Shay's house. Still completely undecided about what to do, I climbed out of the car. The front door was open with just the screen door shut to keep bugs out. I took that as a good sign.

I lightly knocked on the screen door. Mrs. Shay peeked through the kitchen and waved me in. Taking a quick look around as I walked through the living room into the kitchen, I noticed the blinds were open and the room was tidy and inviting.

Mrs. Shay came up to me as I entered the kitchen.

"Hi Tess," she said as she gave me a hug. The hug lasted for a while. I think longer than she intended. I didn't comment or complain. She could close her eyes and hug me and maybe for a split second it would feel like hugging Leigh.

When she pulled back, I could see her eyes watering even though she tried to quickly turn toward the counter to pour me some coffee. I gave her some space and sat down at the kitchen table. She brought a cup of coffee over both of us and sat down.

"Where is Mr. Shay?" I asked.

"He had to go by the funeral home with my sister to help with some arrangements," she replied. "I couldn't bring myself to go," she added quietly.

I reached out and squeezed her hand. I made a mental note to swing by the funeral home to see if there was anything I could do to help. We drank our coffee and the only noise in the kitchen was the morning news coming from the small television on the counter.

"Are you hungry?" she asked, getting up. "Let me fix you some eggs."

"Sure, that sounds good." I wasn't particularly hungry, but she needed something to keep her busy.

"So, how long are you in town for?" she asked.

"Oh, well..." I was caught off guard by her question. "Awhile," I hedged. "I'm back home, living with Benny."

She stopped what she was doing and looked at me with surprise.

"Really? Why now?" she asked.

I wasn't going to get into getting fired and then hearing about Leigh and something inside of me just snapping. I tried to figure out how to respond.

"I don't know," I finally said. "When I heard about Leigh, I didn't really think about it. Honestly, it was almost like I was on autopilot. I started packing up my stuff, got in my car, and left. There was nothing keeping me there."

She nodded and turned back towards the counter and making the eggs.

I drank my coffee, lost in thought. Leigh had tried everything to get me to come home for a weekend. She said I could stay at her house if I didn't want to go to Benny's or we could get a hotel room in Harrisonburg and stay there. She promised to be by my side the whole time. Every holiday, she would ask me to come home.

I never did.

"Leigh was always trying to get you to come home," Mrs. Shay said.

Did all the adults in this town become telepathic while I was away?

"I know. She never gave up on me. She was the best friend anyone could've asked for. I wish I had been a better friend to her."

Mrs. Shay came over and put a plate of scrambled eggs and toast down on the table in front me and then grabbed a plate for herself.

We started eating our breakfast in silence. I don't think either of us really felt like eating, but it gave us something to do.

"Thank you for breakfast," I said after a couple of bites.

"You're welcome." She put her fork down and sat back in her chair.

"Tess, Leigh loved you. She would never give up on you coming home. I wish it didn't take her death to get you to finally do it." Her voice took on a little edge as she got angry.

"I know." The eggs turned to lead in my stomach. I could understand Mrs. Shay's anger with me. Or maybe she wasn't angry with me, just life in general, and needed to get it out.

"You want to come home now and make things right with everyone? My daughter's funeral is not your excuse," she said, her voice rising and getting harder.

"Mrs. Shay, I'm sorry. I'm not trying to cause you any more pain, and I'm definitely not using Leigh's funeral as an excuse to be back. I loved her too. She was the only friend that I would see or stay in touch with over all these years. I promise I'm not trying to disrespect her."

As she was looking at me, the anger drained away like someone pulled a plug on her. She sat back in her chair; she looked defeated. I preferred her anger.

"I came home because I've been doing nothing but surviving all these years. Drifting from one life goal to the next with no real purpose. Checking things off a list. Graduate college, check. Get a job, check. Get an apartment, check. I didn't hang out with friends or have any real relationships. All I did was work all the time. When I heard about Leigh, something clicked in my head and all I could think about was coming home. I wish I had done it a lot sooner." I scooted the quickly congealing eggs around on my plate with my fork.

She sighed and dropped her fork on her plate. "I don't know why I lashed out at you." She got up and walked over to the stove. Grabbing the pan, she threw it in the kitchen sink and started running water and dumping dish soap on it. She turned off the water but didn't leave the kitchen sink. Her shoulders started shaking and I could tell she was crying.

Unsure of what to do, I got up and stood next to her. "Please know that I don't want to do anything to dishonor or take away from Leigh's memory," I whispered. "She was my best friend, and I loved her. One of my biggest regrets is how much time I lost with her."

"She knew you loved her," Mrs. Shay said. "She wanted to make things better for you, even though I told her many times the only one that could make things better for you was you."

"You were right." I grabbed her hand and gently pulled her back to the table to sit down. I picked up our plates and cleaned up the dishes while Mrs. Shay drank her coffee, that had long since gone cold.

After I cleaned the kitchen, I sat down at the table with her again.

"I'm working on Leigh's eulogy. Do you still want me to give it?"

"Yes, of course I do, Tess," she said.

"Do you mind if I grab some things from her room?" I asked. "You will get everything back. There are pictures and some mementos I would like to help with the eulogy."

"Take what you need," she said, patting my hand.

"Why don't you go lay down for a little while?"

"No, I don't feel like laying down anymore."

"Okay." I took her cup and got her more coffee and left her sitting in the kitchen.

I went up the split-level stairs and down the hall to Leigh's bedroom. Stopping outside her room, my hand on the doorknob and my head leaning on the door, I paused and took a deep breath. I had already been in Leigh's room once, but I didn't think that meant it was going to be any easier to go in it again.

Finally, I turned the doorknob and slowly opened the door like you would if someone was sleeping and you didn't want to wake them. God, how I wished that was the case here.

I entered Leigh's pink room reluctantly. Like an invisible force was making me put one foot in front of the other. Running out of the house to get away as fast I can would not make Mrs. Shay feel any better about me. And I had a job to do. Supporting her parents as much as they would let me and doing a proper job with her eulogy was the last thing I could do for my friend. Running, again, would help no one.

Private pep talk for one done; I took a deep breath and got started. It was time to get what I needed and get to work.

# Chapter 11

# COME TO DINNER

*"There isn't time, so brief is life, for bickerings, apologies, heartburnings, callings to account. There is only time for loving, and but an instant, so to speak, for that."*
— Mark Twain

After leaving the Shays, I came home and spent the day going through the pictures and other odds and ends I took from Leigh's room. I added some of my own mementos from over the years growing up together. By the time I was done, I had transformed the living room into a small shrine to Leigh. I sat down and started putting together all the notes and memories I had been jotting down and collecting from other people into some sort of cohesive order. Once I started writing, everything came together to tell the story of Leigh.

By the time I stopped, I had a good first draft, and the light in the room was fading. I knew it had to be well after 6pm which meant I needed to get ready to go to Jack's for dinner. Instead of the nervousness I felt earlier about the entire ordeal, I actually found myself looking forward to it. I had known these people nearly my whole life, and I missed them. Plus, Benny would be there too. I shouldn't depend on my brother to fight my battles, and I didn't, but it was nice to know that someone would be there to have my back if needed. Jack had said he wanted to put the past behind us and move forward, which I'm sure he had told his family by now. The Hallowells would support him in that, even his mom.

With that thought, I cranked up the volume on my 80s hair bands playlist on Spotify and began getting ready. Guns-n-Roses was in the jungle when I got in the shower, and Poison was figuring out roses had thorns when I got out. Glancing out the window, I saw Benny's Jeep in the driveway. Just then, he yelled up the stairs, "Tess, I'll be ready in 20 minutes."

"Okay."

I opened my window and stuck my arm out to check the weather before figuring out what to wear. It was getting into late spring in Virginia which meant it could be hot and in the 80s or cool and in the 60s/70s or cold and in the 50s. Trying to predict Virginia weather between March and May was like trying to predict where the ball was going to land on a roulette wheel. The only thing that was predictable was when summer finally hit us for good, she hit us hard. Muggy, hot, and humid weather would be here soon enough. I would take the unpredictable spring over the always stifling summer any time.

A cool breeze blew in and carried with it the sweet smell of the honeysuckle that climbed the side of the house under my window. It would be a nice night. Grabbing a pair of jeans and an ivory colored, long-sleeve peasant top, I quickly got dressed. Completing the look with a pair of brown wedge sandals, I checked my outfit in the mirror. Not wanting to look overdone, I left my hair down and put on a little light makeup. I did not want to look like I was trying to dress for a date. This was a family dinner, nothing more.

Benny and I hopped in his Jeep with ten minutes to spare for the three-minute drive to the Hallowell's. We pulled into the driveway and parked in one of the few spots left. Everyone must be home for dinner. The house was lit up with light shining out of every window.

A nervous excitement coursed through me. I looked at Benny and hoped I didn't look like a deer in the headlights. He gave me an encouraging smile before he got out of the Jeep and opened my door. My dad always did that for my mom and me, and he taught Benny to always do the same.

"Ready?" he asked as he grabbed my hand to help me out in my sandals.

"Yes, I am."

We headed to the house and knocked on the screen door, as the front door was wide open, as always. It could be 90 degrees in the shade in summer or 20 degrees and snowing in the winter, but the Hallowell's front door was always open.

"Since when do you people knock?" yelled Max from the couch in the living room where he was watching television. "Get in here."

Benny opened the screen door as Mr. Hallowell came out of the kitchen.

"Tess," he said, giving me a hug. "We have missed you."

"I've missed you all too."

"Benny," Mr. Hallowell said, reaching out to shake my brother's hand.

"Hi Mr. Hallowell. Thank you for having us over for dinner."

"Of course, you and Tess are always welcome here."

Max came up and flung his arm around my shoulders. "Good to see you messy Tessy."

I rolled my eyes. Max called me messy Tessy the first time he met me when we were kids and apparently was never going to stop. I tried to give him an annoyed glare, but I couldn't hold on to it when looking at his good-natured, smiling face.

"How have you been, Max?" We headed into the kitchen, followed by Benny and Mr. Hallowell. Remembering what Benny told me this morning, I tried to look for anything different about Max, maybe something I never noticed growing up, but he seemed to be the same happy person as always. He must have perfected hiding what was going on beneath the surface. I idly wondered if he could teach me how. I seemed to do the exact opposite and broadcast what I was feeling to everyone.

"I've been good. Did a stint in the rodeo for a short time but I'm home now and helping TJ get this horse business off the ground," he said.

I nodded, but before I could say anything in response, we were in the kitchen with the rest of the family. TJ and Nick rose from the large kitchen table as we entered, and Mrs. Hallowell stopped chopping potatoes at the kitchen counter.

Great, she's got a knife, I thought wryly.

Benny and I greeted TJ and Nick with handshakes and hugs. All the Hallowell men were roughly six feet tall, give or take an inch, and towered over Benny and me. I was just about to ask where Jack was when he came into the kitchen.

He was wearing jeans and a long sleeve Henley shirt that showed off his very strong shoulders. I couldn't help but notice. His hair was wet and tousled from the shower. All he did was run his hands through it. He didn't bother using something as troublesome as a brush. If I remember correctly, I don't think he ever actually owned a brush. Must be nice to always have that perfectly messy hair that looks so good on guys.

"Hey Benny," he said, shaking my brother's hand and clapping him on the shoulder as he made his way into the kitchen.

"Hi Tess," he said, giving me a hug. His hair had a woodsy, minty smell that was pleasant, not overpowering. You had to be close enough to notice.

Benny and Jack's brothers went into the living room to watch television, which left me alone with Jack and his parents. His mom still hadn't said the first word to me.

Mr. Hallowell sat down at the kitchen table.

"Have a seat Tess, tell us how you've been doing," he said invitingly. I glanced at Mrs. Hallowell but couldn't read her expression. I think she was trying very hard to not show what she was thinking.

"Is there anything I can do to help with dinner?" I asked her.

"No, dinner is covered," she said. "Just finishing cutting the potatoes for boiling."

"Okay," I said quietly and walked over to sit at the table with Mr. Hallowell. Jack sat down next to me. I could feel the tension in the room despite Jack and his dad trying to keep the mood light and friendly.

I wasn't sure of the best way to proceed with Mrs. Hallowell. A lot of people did not like her. But they didn't know her. Most of the people in town considered her to be stubborn, demanding, and unforgiving. To be effective at managing the business end of a farm, she had to be. Suppliers will feed you every excuse in the book for why an order was late, short, or not there at all. Customers always wanted more and more, but to pay less and less. While I was growing up, I'd watched how she managed it all; she even taught me how to do some of that part of the business over the years. Managing all the various customers and suppliers for a farm could easily be a full-time job. She did it while also raising four boys and pitching in with the hard outdoor labor that was needed, too.

One thing everyone could agree on, she was fiercely protective of her family. That encompassed more than just her boys and husband. Anyone she had welcomed into her home and life was her family because she didn't do that easily or often. But she did it for Benny and me. She had treated us no differently than her own kids growing up. My mom was one of the few women she called a friend. By nature, Mrs. Hallowell didn't easily make friends or let people get close.

She let me in and let me get close and I hurt one of her boys. Badly. I wondered if we could ever get back to where we were before. Had I permanently damaged our relationship?

"What kind of work did you do in Arlington?" Mr. Hallowell asked, to break the silence that had taken over the kitchen.

I tore my eyes away from Mrs. Hallowell. She had turned her back on me and gone back to cutting her potatoes.

"I worked for a little restaurant called The Olive Tree. An Italian restaurant. I was with them from the beginning when they first opened. I became friends with the owner Vito. I was assistant manager," I replied.

"Wow, that's really cool Tess," he said. "Will you have to get back soon for work?"

The pit of my stomach turned. I guess it was a bit of a miracle no one had asked about work before now. Everyone was preoccupied with so many other things going on between Leigh's funeral, Benny and his business, Ruby's illness. My employment, or lack thereof, was not top of mind. I saw Benny glance at me a couple of times like he wanted to ask if I was working or a job was going to miss me eventually but he seemed to sense that I did not want to discuss it. His brotherly intuition was on point.

"Noooo," I said with a bit of hesitation. "I'm no longer working there."

It was on the tip of my tongue to say I may have another opportunity, but I wasn't ready to get into the offer in New York and should I or shouldn't I. Of course, what I want is not going to stop Mrs. Hallowell from going straight to the point.

"So, what do you plan on doing then?" Mrs. Hallowell asked from the other side of the kitchen, startling me a bit.

"I've got some ideas, but I'm still trying to figure that out," I hedged. "I have some money saved up, but I don't want to eat up all my savings, so I will need to figure out something soon. For the time being, though,

I'm focused on helping Benny write a business plan for the shop. And writing Leigh's eulogy."

Mrs. Hallowell didn't respond with more than a nod of her head to acknowledge she heard me. She put the pot of potatoes on the stove to boil and joined us at the kitchen table.

"So, you've finally decided the world doesn't stop because of Tess?" she asked.

The blood drained from my face at her harsh words. I had heard Mrs. Hallowell let people have it over the years but had never been on the receiving end. I really wanted to get up and run out of that kitchen and never look back, but that would be the worst thing I could do. Running away and not looking back caused most of the pain and damage to my most important relationships. If I wanted to fix my relationship with Mrs. Hallowell, I had to stand up for myself and fight back. She would never respect me again if I didn't.

"Mom," Jack said heatedly. "I told you to give her a chance and not be like this when she got here."

Mr. Hallowell reached over and grabbed his wife's hand. "Jenny," he said quietly, but nothing more. I thought it was probably pretty wise of him to stop there and learned from much experience.

I swallowed, took a deep breath, and sat up straighter in my chair. I felt like I was preparing to do battle with Lancelot and I was nothing but an untrained squire.

"It's okay Jack. I know as well as you do you can't tell your mom to do anything, especially in her own house."

"Would it be okay for you and me to talk alone?" I asked her. She looked a little surprised; maybe a little pleased, but that might have been wishful thinking on my part.

"We can," she said and gave Jack and Mr. Hallowell a look and a nod. Gladly taking the hint, they made a beeline for the living room to watch television with the others.

Mrs. Hallowell sat silently after they left. I had asked for this conversation with her alone and she was waiting for me to start.

"I know I hurt many people after my parents died. I didn't handle it well. I was angry." I paused here, trying to collect my thoughts. She gave me time and said nothing. "That doesn't excuse the way I treated everyone, especially Jack."

"Have you ever heard of the five stages of grief?" she asked, catching me off guard.

"Ummm, no," I said, a little shocked.

"I wanted to understand what was going on with you and how we could help."

"You did?" I was more than a little surprised.

I wouldn't think Mrs. Hallowell put much stock in the whole mental health movement. She was more of a suck it up and move on type of person. If you told her you were depressed, she would roll her eyes, tell you to eat a donut, and go do some bush hogging. She was of the mind that physical labor could make anyone feel better, probably because it worked for her. Truthfully, she wasn't entirely wrong. It's well known that exercise goes a long way in helping people with their mental health. I'd wondered many times over the years if I had stuck with my running routine during that whole time, maybe I would have handled things better.

Wishing I could take back the past and get a do over would not get me anywhere though.

"There are five stages of grief - denial, anger, bargaining, depression, and acceptance," she continued. "It's not a hard and fast rule, but generally, these are what most people go through after an immense loss in their life. There is no timeline for each stage and no map for how to get someone who seems stuck in one stage over the hump and moving onto the next stage."

She paused and took a sip of her coffee. I was a little shocked, not knowing how to respond. This was so out of character of the woman I thought I knew.

"Best I could tell, you were stuck between denial and anger. Honestly, I'm probably one of the few people that thought you did the right thing when you packed your crap and left. I don't think you realized it at the time, or even now, but you were protecting yourself. You needed to get out of here, I think. Needed a change of scenery, a change of people. I'm not some damn therapist or anything, but I know what it's like to want to just lash out, get the anger out, and maybe make people hurt because you hurt. And you can't deal with all that hurt."

"Problem is, you hurt Jack," she continued. "That's where I have a hard time. I had to keep away from you after that whole prom scene. I understood your lashing out, probably better than most, but I couldn't forgive that. At least, not right away. But, it was a long time ago and Jack is a grown man now. You're grown now. I'm not going to hold onto some grudge I had against a traumatized kid years ago." She picked up her coffee and took a big gulp to finish it off. "Anybody that does hold onto that grudge is an asshole and you don't need them anyway."

If someone smacked me with a feather, it would've knocked me out of my chair at this point. I've known Mrs. Hallowell since the second grade, nearly my whole life. My parents were friends with her. She was Jack's mom. She had been as much a part of raising me as my uncle, Ms. Ruby, and, of course, my parents. She was the image of a strong woman who would call it like she saw it and did not have time to worry about hurting feelings.

How many people had seen the side to her I'm seeing now?

I thought about what she had just said about the stages of grief and mental health. When Jack and I were kids, his grandmother passed away. She lived with the family and helped raise the boys. They were all very close to her. It was hard on all the boys but I think especially Jack. They always seemed to have a special bond, I think because of Jack's photography.

Of course, I never realized it as a kid but the boys didn't just lose a grandmother.

"When you lost your mom?" I asked.

"Not just my mom," she said. "I lost my dad when I was eight to cancer. My grandmother moved in with my mom and me. Then we lost Grandma when I was 16. And then my mom died when you were around 12 and Jack was 13."

"I remember," I whispered.

She looked at me and let me see the grief she still carried. It showed on her face, plain as day. The number of people she allowed to see this side of her were few and could probably be counted on one hand.

"You'll carry the grief with you always," she said. "But it does get ... less. I found what helped the most was having the people I cared about around me. I did the same as you at first. After my dad died, I acted out, got in fights at school, ran away a couple of times, and did whatever I could to push people away, including my mom and grandmother. I was young and in so much pain that I didn't know how to handle."

I sat in silence and listened, scared that if I made any sudden movements or even breathed too loudly, she would clam up and stop talking. I always thought I knew Mrs. Hallowell. She praised me, scolded me, taught me as if I was one of her own growing up. She loved her boys fiercely and would do anything for them, but I think she liked the idea of having a little girl to bring up too.

But I knew her as a child knows an adult. She was this all-knowing being that had all the answers. She was never sad or depressed. I don't think I'd ever seen her cry once the entire time I've known her. Even at her mom's funeral. Now, I was getting to know her like an adult knows another adult. The child, adult relationship was over. It was time to move onto something more mature. Something that had a little more depth of understanding.

"A teacher at my school reached out to my mom and told her she thought it would be good for me to talk to a therapist. Back then, needing therapy and taking care of your mental health wasn't something that was discussed. If you needed therapy, you were crazy." She rolled her eyes. "Mental health is just as important as physical. Even today, people think of it as two separate things. You are not just a body, so why people would think that's all that needs professional help is beyond me."

"My mom got in contact with a counselor at the high school that my teacher recommended. Besides working as a counselor at the school, he worked as a grief counselor and led support groups. I started meeting with him up to three times a week at first. It took a long time but slowly, I came around. I had to make that happen, though. No one can do it for you. Therapists, friends, family, they can all help but, at the end of the day, it's you that has to do the work. You have to decide you will not be beat by the grief and lose who you are because of it."

Flashes of memory came back to me of the time after my parents' deaths. Mrs. Hallowell showing up randomly at the house to bring Benny and me some food she made and make sure everything was clean and in working order.

I was lying on the couch after school one day, staring at the television without really listening to whatever was on. She came over and sat down with me and just held my hand. She didn't say anything, and neither did I. She sat there until Benny came home from work. The next week she came over after school and I was laying in the same spot on the couch. She turned off the television, and I stared at the blank screen, not really caring that it was off.

"Tess, you need to talk to someone. A counselor at the school, a teacher, me, I don't care. You can't keep going on like this."

I said nothing to her. I just got up and went upstairs to my room and left her sitting in the living room by herself. Not to be deterred, Mrs. Hallowell didn't give up. She kept coming over; she even called the school and had the counselors try to talk to me. No one was getting through to me, though, because I didn't want them to break through those walls. Those walls were holding back the hurt. The anger and lashing out at people was protecting me from having to feel the crushing pain every time someone talked about my parents.

When I was in the middle of it, I never thought that Mrs. Hallowell was trying to help me and might know what I was going through. I had the self-centered mentality of a child that still didn't realize adults were people, too. It didn't occur to me I had been to her mother's funeral. That she might understand the pain. She kept trying to get through to me until the night of Jack's prom. After that, she stopped. She loved me; I knew that, even then. I actually never questioned it. But I had crushed and humiliated one of her boys, and that was a step too far.

Now, sitting across from her in this kitchen drinking coffee and seeing her with an adult's eyes, I realize I am just starting to know this woman who has so much more depth to her character than I think me or most people in our small town ever gave her credit for.

"It took a long time, a lot of counseling, and probably growing up and becoming more mature for me to really learn how to handle the grief. I was a daddy's girl through and through. Losing him upended my whole world. I had to learn how to live again after he was gone," she said.

She stopped talking and put her empty coffee cup that she had been twisting around in her hand down on the table. "I shouldn't have stopped trying to get through to you after the whole prom fiasco. That was wrong of me. I am sorry for that."

"You're apologizing to me?" I said incredulously. Not in a million years with a million different scenarios to choose from would I have ever thought that this was how this evening was going to go. "Mrs. Hallowell, you have nothing to apologize for. You and your family have always been amazing to me, and Jack was and still is one of my closest friends. I hate remembering that night and knowing how horrible I was to him. I wish I could take it all back, but as that's impossible, all I can do is try to make things right now and move forward."

She grimaced. "Well, normally, if a girl treated one of my boys like that, I'd hunt her down and make her wish she never met me." She sighed. "But I've known you most of your life. I know your family. And I know you care for Jack. Whether you are friends or something more, I know you care for him either way," she said, shrugging like it was a fact of life. Because it was.

"I love him." I looked her in the eyes. "I know that we've been apart for years and things did not end well between us. But I never stopped loving him. I always have loved him since that day on the playground when he told the other kids to shut their pie holes and let me play." The memory still made me smile. Mrs. Hallowell laughed and the sadness that she had been wearing through the conversation melted away.

"Jack's one of my best friends. We may never be more than friends again, but I will always love him," I said.

Just then, Jack strolled into the kitchen like it was just another day, and he didn't have a care in the world. I felt a little drained after such an intense conversation with his mom. But, at least, the anxiety I'd been having about seeing Mrs. Hallowell was gone.

"Everything okay?" he asked.

I knew he had to hear at least the tail end of our conversation. How I felt about him wasn't exactly a secret, but it's still a little embarrassing to have the man you are talking about walk into the room when you are talking about him. I looked at his mom and knew I definitely looked like a deer in the headlights now. She tried to hide her face behind her coffee cup and cover her laugh with a cough.

Jack walked over to me and crouched down next to my chair. He put his arm around my shoulders and kissed my cheek. "Just wanted to make sure you two are good again," he said, reaching over to his mom's hand and patting it. Then he stood up and went back to the living room.

Mrs. Hallowell and I sat silently for a moment. I wasn't sure what I was feeling, but butterflies started having a field day in my stomach. It felt like he just opened the door a little more to the possibility of being something more.

Mrs. Hallowell reached over and patted my hand. "How about a glass of wine? Dinner should be done soon."

I nodded. "That sounds great. I'll set the table." I walked over and grabbed the dishes out of the cabinet and the silverware from the drawer. She handed me a pile of napkins on my way to the dining room.

# Chapter 12

# BACK PORCH CONVERSATIONS

*"He is more myself, Than I am. Whatever our souls are made of, His and mine are the same."*
— Emily Bronte

"Wow, look at all the stars. Living in Arlington, I think I forgot how beautiful a night sky is when there's not a bunch of light pollution messing it up," I said.

Jack and I were sitting on the back porch after dinner. Everyone else had been sitting out here with us, but one by one, they seemed to find something else to do. T.J., Nick, Max, and Benny were inside playing pool and Mr. And Mrs. Hallowell went to watch the nightly news and get ready for bed. Now, it was just Jack and me.

"I guess it is something we take for granted around here," Jack responded.

We sat in comfortable silence, each lost in our own thoughts. He was nursing a beer, and I was sipping on my second glass of wine. Dinner felt like old times. Everyone seemed to collectively agree that it was time to let the past rest. It felt like I had just had dinner with the family last week instead of the years that it had actually been since I'd shared a meal with them. Still, as comfortable and familiar as it all was, there was a sadness that blanketed the evening. Leigh hadn't been at the Hallowell's as much as me growing up, but she had been there enough for the whole family to feel her loss. Still, dinner had been fun, lively, and full of conversations just like always at the Hallowell's.

"So, do you plan on staying here for a while then? Like moving back?" Mr. Hallowell asked me as he passed me the chicken.

"Well, yes, I guess I kind of already did. I didn't have any furniture as it all came with the apartment, so I only had clothes and stuff to move. I packed up everything that night. The night I found out about Leigh."

He put his hand over mine in a fatherly gesture. His hands were rough from years of hard labor on the farm, but his touch was gentle. "I'm so sorry," he said simply. I nodded and held his hand for a minute. It reminded me of my dad's.

"We are all here for you if you need anything, Tess," Mrs. Hallowell said. She was sitting on the other side of Mr. Hallowell.

"Thanks, I appreciate it. I've made a lot of progress on the eulogy, but I need to get it done. I may come by and read it to you. Let me know what you think of it. If I need to change anything."

"Absolutely," she said and then changed the subject, for which I was very grateful. I had been holding it together ever since finding out about Leigh and I really didn't want to fall apart sitting at the dinner table. I think all the other complications of coming home had preoccupied me. Facing the people I had hurt and trying to make things right had been a distraction. Now that I had reconnected with most of those people, that anxiety and worry that had been acting like a shield was going away. Thoughts and memories of Leigh were coming through and taking over. I was feeling her loss worse now than when I first heard about her death.

"How is our new baby doing?" Mrs. Hallowell asked Max.

That snapped me out of my thoughts. "New baby?" I asked.

"Not a baby baby," Max said, grinning.

"The way you run around, I wouldn't be so sure," Nick joked, earning him a sharp look from Mrs. Hallowell, but she directed her attention to Max.

"Maximilian Hallowell, you better not be running around like that," she said. "I did not raise my boys to think they can behave that way."

"I don't," Max said, holding his hands up like he was waiting on her to shoot him right there at the table. He very obviously kicked Nick under the table. Nick just chuckled and went back to his dinner.

Jack was next to me, and I gave him a questioning look. He just raised his eyebrows and kept eating. That look said it would be best not to comment on Max's "running around."

To take the heat off Max, I asked, "So, who is the new baby?"

"One of the mares had a foal about two weeks ago," he said.

From then on, the dinner conversation was taken over with talk about horses, the planting schedule, and other farm matters. Mr. Hallowell asked Benny about the shop and Uncle Rob, and we discussed the business plan I was creating for them for a bit. Dinner with the Hallowell's was like putting on your favorite well-worn sweatshirt and pajama pants. It was comfortable and familiar. I could feel the tension I had been feeling for the past few days easing little by little.

After cleaning up from dinner, we had all come out to the back porch to relax and watch the last vestiges of light fade away to darkness. I was sitting on the top step, leaning against the railing and facing Jack. He was leaning against the opposite railing, facing me.

"Do you still do your photography?" I asked, breaking the silence. "I saw some new photos hanging around the house. Are they yours?"

"Yeah," he replied. "I'm still at. I built a website and have sold a few photos."

"Oh my goodness, that's great, Jack!" I said excitedly. It had always been his dream to get into photography.

He shrugged. "It's a good hobby and puts a little a extra cash in my pocket."

"I know you have the farm and your family here, but did you ever consider trying to make a go of photography full-time? As a career?" I asked.

"Of course I have, but it's kind of my escape, you know," he said. "If it becomes my job, I wonder if I would love it as much." He shrugged again and took another sip of beer. "Besides, the future isn't written in stone. Who knows what happens down the road? For now, I'm happy with working on the farm and doing the photography thing on the side."

"What about you?" he asked. "I mean, I know you just got back and are dealing with Leigh's funeral and trying to help her family. But what comes after that?"

I shrugged and sighed. Now was probably as good a time as any to talk about New York. I needed to tell someone and talk about what I wanted to do. But the words wouldn't come. I don't know what was holding me back from bring it up to anyone or really even thinking about it. "For now, I'm focused on helping Benny with the things he wants to do at the shop. It's the least I can do after everything he's done for me. He pretty much put his life on hold to raise me. Who knows what plans and dreams he had before our parents died and he got stuck with raising a depressed and moody teenager?"

"You? Moody? No," he said jokingly. "Calling you 'moody' is like calling ..."

Laughing, I kicked him with my foot. "Be careful finishing that thought," I joked.

"In all seriousness, Benny would be hurt if he thought you felt like you owed him," he said. "He could have easily let Rob or Ms. Ruby take you, they both offered, but you were his sister. He wanted you with him."

I felt so much love and appreciation for everything my brother did for me. I wanted to help him as much for me as for him.

He slid across the step and pulled me to him so we were sitting side by side and he put his arm around my shoulders. I laid my head against his shoulder. "It's not that I feel like I owe him, although I do. I just want to help him. I want to show him I can be there for him like he was for me," I said. "Does that make sense?"

"Yeah, that makes sense."

We sat on the steps and watched the fireflies dancing in the yard. We didn't talk. It was a little cooler outside now that night had finally taken over completely, but it was still warm enough to be comfortable. In some sense, it felt like nothing had changed between us. But we couldn't completely ignore the past or sweep the years that I had been away under the rug. We both grew and changed over those years. Pretending they didn't happen would not help us rebuild our friendship.

After a few minutes, I lifted my head off his shoulders and pulled away, putting some space between us.

"So, besides work, what else have you been up to?" I asked quietly. "Do you have a girlfriend?"

Jack was good-looking, smart, and charming. There was no way he hadn't had at least a couple of girlfriends while I was away. Heck, he could have a fiancée for all I knew, but I doubted no one would've mentioned that since I've been back.

He shrugged. "I've dated here and there and had some relationships that lasted a couple of months but, mostly, nothing stuck. There was one, though, that could have worked out. She was a grad student and teacher's assistant at JMU. I met her when I was taking some classes in photography."

"What happened?" I asked.

"She graduated and didn't want to stick around here. Max was still recovering from his rodeo accident. Dad and T.J. were trying to get us into the horse business, too. It wasn't a great time for me to leave the farm and follow her. I would've been leaving my family in the lurch, which I would never do for anyone," he said. "Plus, I love it here. I don't want to live somewhere else. At least not now. But, like I said, you never know what the future holds."

I nodded. "No, you definitely don't," I said. "I'm sorry she didn't want to stick around, at least until it would've been a better time for you to consider leaving."

"It is what it is. I don't blame her. She worked hard to get where she is and there wasn't going to be a lot of opportunity around here for her."

"Do you keep in touch?" I asked.

"Not really," he replied. "There were a couple of phone calls here and there at first, but that stopped after about a month or two. We're friends on Facebook but I'm hardly ever on it, so I don't know if that counts as keeping in touch."

I laughed a little. "Probably not, Jack."

He smiled at me. "So, what about you? Did you find Prince Charming while you were away?"

I smiled back at him. "Ha ha. No, there were no Prince Charmings. I kept to myself a lot at Tech. I tried doing the partying thing. See if I could snap out of it and feel like myself again. Turns out, drinking and partying wasn't going to be the way."

"No?" he said, faking shock.

I rolled my eyes. "My junior year, I talked to one of the school counselors."

"Did it help?" he asked.

I shrugged. "It may have if I would've kept up with it. I would go a couple of times, and then drop off and not go for a month, and then go again once or twice, and then drop off again."

"I was shutting people out and closing myself off. Logically, I knew this wasn't healthy. The few people that I would hang out with or talk to tried to get me to go out or do something outside of class, but they stopped trying after a while. I thought about dropping out for a while there."

"That probably wouldn't have solved anything."

"I know, and I didn't want to come back home. I was ashamed how I had treated everyone. How I left things. I didn't have it in me to come back and fix it. At any rate, I also knew that running away from Tech wasn't going to fix anything or be good for my future."

I stopped for a minute. Trying to collect my thoughts and explain the place I was in. Jack sat quietly, giving me time.

"I made it through sophomore year and started working at one of the local restaurants over the summer. Instead of being a server like most of the college kids, I worked in the kitchen. I learned to do prep work and helped work the line. I loved it. It kept me busy, and I felt like my old self again for just a little while. I became friends with some of the people I worked with. It was good."

"Going into junior year, I changed my major to restaurant and hospitality management. I also took some night classes in cooking through junior and senior year. When I was cooking, I felt like me again. It had been a long time since I felt like me," I mumbled, more to myself than to Jack. "I graduated and got the job at Vito's restaurant. I moved to Arlington and have been living there ever since."

"Until I left it all in the middle of the night and moved back in with Benny a few days ago. I might need to stop packing up and leaving in the middle of the night," I joked half-heartedly.

"No kidding. I need to talk to Benny about putting a lock on your door at night or something."

I laughed.

"It sounds like you found something you really like," he said.

I nodded. "Cooking and working at The Olive Tree may have been my Prince Charming. I'm not saying it saved me, but it was the first time I felt..." I struggled for the right word to explain it. "Better, I guess. I'm not the same person I was before my parents died. I doubt I ever will be, but cooking made me want to be out in the world again."

"I feel the same about photography. It's my escape. When I'm looking through a camera, everything else just fades away and all I think about is capturing what I'm trying to take a picture of, all of it. The essence of it," he said.

"I was looking at some photos hanging inside. You've gotten a lot better since high school. You really are talented."

"Thanks." He stared at the ground, lost in thought. "For a time there, after we broke up and then when you moved away, when I wasn't working on the farm or in class, it was practically all I did. It helped me get through everything."

I reached over and tentatively touched his hand. "I'm sorry," I whispered.

He slowly turned his hand over so he could hold mine, staring down at where we touched. I slowly scooted back over so I was sitting close to him again.

"Dating your best friend can be great while things are going well," he said. "But when things go south, it's so much worse. I didn't just lose a girlfriend; I lost my best friend. I was lost and it took a long time for me to get through it. Deep down, I knew the pain I was feeling was just a fraction of the pain you were feeling from your parents' deaths. In a way, it helped me to understand. I just wanted you to be happy. If you had to do that away from here, then so be it."

"I wish I hadn't hurt everyone the way I did, though," I said.

He shrugged. "It was years ago, Tess. You were young and dealing with a lot of pain that most people don't have to deal with until they are much older. No one knows how they will react to something like that. All you can hope for is some understanding and forgiveness from your friends and family while you work through it. I don't think anyone is going to hold it against you or not want you around."

"Everyone has been really great since I've been back, actually. Ms. Ruby was a little miffed about me leaving for school in the middle of the night, but she understood why I did it. I was nervous about how Uncle Rob would be when I went to see him, but he was great."

"I think we're all glad you are back again, and you seem happier," he said. "No one is going to hold anything against you, Tess. And if they do, they are being ridiculous, and you don't need them."

I smiled at him. We sat on these same back porch steps for years growing up, talking, playing cards, listening to music, just hanging out. The day after our first kiss by the campfire, I came over to his house and we sat on these steps drinking his mom's iced tea and talking. He told me he wanted to take me out, wanted me to be his girlfriend, but he didn't want to lose his best friend. I had promised him he would never lose me as a friend, no matter what.

But you never know what the future holds.

We were still holding hands.

"It's getting late," I said. "Benny and I will need to go soon."

"I know."

I went to stand up, but he held onto me and pulled me back to the steps.

"What do you think about you and I going out one night?" he asked, looking into my eyes. His hair was blowing just a little in the slight breeze.

I didn't want to hurt him again. "As friends or something more?"

"I'm not sure. Maybe we go out and find out where it leads."

"I don't want to hurt you again. I just got back and I'm still trying to figure things out."

"I'll pay," he said, smiling.

I laughed. "I didn't say I was broke."

"I'm not trying to rush into anything. Let's just hang out, me and you. No brothers or parents around. We don't need to define it right now."

I took a breath. "That sounds perfect, actually," I said. "But not until after the funeral. Leigh is always at the back of my mind and maybe always will be, but I think I'll enjoy hanging out more after the funeral is done."

Thinking about her funeral always brought a fresh wave of sadness and anxiety. My best girlfriend was gone, and her family was depending on me to do the eulogy. "I miss her so much," I whispered.

He put his arm around me and pulled me to him. "Me too."

We sat quietly together, each lost in our own thoughts about Leigh, until Benny came out on the back porch. "Hey Tess, you about ready to go?"

"Yeah." I stood up with a sigh and stretched.

Jack got up too. "Let me know if you need any help with Leigh's eulogy, the Shays, or the funeral arrangements," he said.

"I will. Thanks for having us over for dinner." I gave him a brief hug.

Benny shook his hand. "Thanks, man."

"See you soon," he said.

"See you soon."

Benny and I walked to the Jeep. I looked back and gave Jack a wave as I got in. He stood on the back porch and watched us drive away.

# Chapter 13

# THE VIEWING

*"The story of life is quicker than the wink of an eye, the story of love is hello and goodbye...until we meet again."*
— **Jimi Hendrix**

The room brightened around me. I could see it even though I didn't open my eyes. The sunlight was poking me, telling me it was time to start the day. I was steadfastly ignoring it. I had been laying in bed for a while. Maybe if I didn't open my eyes and acknowledge the daylight, time would stand still, and this day wouldn't happen. The covers on my bed were soft and comforting and part of me wanted to hide under them and never come out.

Leigh's viewing was today. Her funeral was tomorrow.

Whatever I was feeling, her parents had to be feeling a hundred times worse. They had to say goodbye to their only child. They would never see their daughter get married, never have grandchildren to spoil, holidays, birthdays, Mondays through Sundays, would never be the same. I knew they were feeling a pain that most wouldn't wish on their worst enemy.

I opened my eyes. Sunlight streaked across the room. Slowly, I sat up and got out of bed. I needed to get dressed and get over to the Shays' house. I wanted to check on them before heading to the funeral home.

I had things to set up before the viewing tonight. Jack and some of our friends from high school were meeting me there.

"Hey Tessie, you up?" Benny yelled up the stairs.

"Yes, I'm almost ready," I yelled back and rushed around, grabbing my clothes. Jeans and t-shirt would be fine for now. I would shower and change before the viewing tonight.

"Okay, coffee is done, and I made some eggs and toast. Eat something."

I smiled despite the sadness. Benny was such a mother hen, but I was grateful for it. I could appreciate it now more than I did when we were younger. He was going with me today. Uncle Rob was going to run the shop for half a day and close early. It would be closed all day tomorrow for the funeral.

I dressed quickly and did a quick scrub of my teeth and face, put my hair in a ponytail, and I was ready. How I looked wasn't my top priority today. Truth be told, it rarely was a priority for me. Even in my 'tween and teen years, I was happy with a ponytail and t-shirts and rarely wore makeup. Leigh was always making me sit through makeovers, though. She loved doing hair and makeup.

The memories crashed into me while I was sitting on the edge of the bed and putting on my Chucks. I smiled despite the fresh wave of sadness that washed over me.

"Tess, would you hold still!" Leigh said in exasperation. She was trying to put eyeliner on my eyes. It tickled like hell.

"I'm about to rub my eyes out and ruin all the perfection you're trying to create," I said, acting annoyed even though I wasn't. Leigh had been using me as her very own living dress-up doll since we met. Leigh's mom came into the room to see how the progress was coming.

"Wow, Tess, you look great," she said, trying to hide her laughter. She wasn't hiding it well.

"Thanks Mrs. Shay," I said wryly. Leigh had curlers in my straight-as—a-board-hair. She had been trying to get my hair to curl for ten years with zero success. The girl was relentless. I would give her that. I had one eye done with makeup and Leigh was now working on the other.

"Leigh, seriously, we're just going to the movies and having dinner at the food court in the mall," I said. "Is this really necessary?" It was Saturday night, and we had finally convinced our parents that we were old enough to go to the mall and hang out without them or Benny as chaperone.

"Yes!" she said incredulously, like I had lost my mind. "Everyone from school will be hanging out there."

"Leigh, we see them nearly every day. They know what I look like without makeup and curly hair."

"Just sit still Tess, I'm almost done." She was lying. I knew she was lying because she always said she was almost done when I got impatient, but I would still be sitting there for another twenty minutes while she got the look "just right."

The memory faded as I finished putting on my shoes and looked around my bedroom. Despite the bright sunshine streaking through the room, it seemed gloomy. Or maybe I was projecting my mood.

I stood in front of the mirror and sighed. I could almost see Leigh's look of disapproval at the offensive ponytail. "Don't worry Leigh, I'm going to do my makeup and hair for tonight and tomorrow. I will look just right for you," I whispered into the empty room.

The smell of coffee hit me as I headed downstairs. Benny was in the kitchen scooping scrambled eggs onto our plates. I grabbed two coffee cups from the cabinet and poured us each a cup putting creamer in mine and sugar in Benny's. Neither of us spoke as we sat down at the table. I really didn't have any kind of appetite. As much as I loved coffee, I didn't know if I could even drink that this morning. My stomach was in knots. Benny didn't look like he was doing a lot better. He moved the eggs around on his plate with his fork, but I hadn't seen him take a bite yet.

"Let's at least try to eat the toast," he finally said after another minute of moving eggs that were getting colder by the second around his plate. We each picked up our toast that was heavy on the butter and ate. It actually helped calm my stomach a bit.

After breakfast, I texted our cousin Kelly to let her know we were heading out. She had been a couple of years ahead of Leigh and me at school, but we had all hung out occasionally and played together as kids. She and some other people from school were meeting us at the funeral home to get things ready for tonight. We had pictures blown up to poster-size, thanks to one friend who worked at a printing press. Another created a slide show with music. People brought their laptops and iPads so we could spread them around the funeral home and have all the Brat Pack movies playing on a loop. I had scoured every nursery, flower shop, grocery store, and Walmart within a reasonable driving distance to buy every pink tulip I could find. They were all laid gently in coolers in the back of Benny's Jeep along with a box of mason jars for vases.

Leigh loved pink tulips. I used to give her a hard time about buying pink tulips whenever she saw them for sale. They always were dead within a couple of days. I told her it was a waste to spend her money on something so delicate with such a short lifespan. She always replied the same way. "Some of the most beautiful things in this world don't have long to live. All the more reason, we need to appreciate their beauty while they are here."

I stared out the window of Benny's Jeep on the way to the Shays as Leigh's words echoed in my head. They rang so true now and had taken on all new meaning for me. I wondered if, on some level, she knew she was not long for this world. Maybe God can only spare the most beautiful things for a short time before he has to call them home.

Benny pulled into the Shays driveway and put the Jeep in park. We sat for a moment, staring at her house. He grabbed my hand and gave it a squeeze. I also had an all-new appreciation for my brother. In his own quiet way, he had always been my rock, giving me strength when I needed it.

"Let's do this," I said.

"Let's do this," he responded.

Mrs. Shay opened the door before we knocked. She looked tired, and I knew she had slept little. Her eyes had dark circles around them, though she made a good effort to cover it with makeup. She was dressed in light pink jeans and a darker pink rose-colored t-shirt.

"Hey Tess," she said quietly, pulling me in for a hug. Then she grabbed Benny and hugged him, too.

Mr. Shay came out of the kitchen and went in for a handshake with Benny as soon as Mrs. Shay let him go. He was wearing a light pink button-down shirt with jeans and a pink bracelet on his wrist. I recognized it from when Leigh and I were kids and made friendship bracelets for everyone. He must have kept it all these years.

"Hey Benny, it's good to see you."

"Mr. Shay." Benny shook his hand.

"Thank you both for everything," Mrs. Shay said.

"We loved her," I said simply. There wasn't anything else to say.

"I put some things you asked for in her car and warmed it up this morning since we haven't started it in a couple of days," Mr. Shay said, handing me the keys to Leigh's Volkswagen Beetle. It was pink with flowers. Leigh really had her own signature style. There was no mistaking it for anyone else.

"Thanks. Is there anything you need before we go?" I asked. They both looked like they hadn't slept in a week and were holding on by a thread.

"My sister is on her way," Mrs. Shay said. "We're keeping it together. Don't worry."

I nodded my head and gave her a small smile. "I know but call me if you need something. Is your sister going to drive you to the viewing or do you want us to come pick you up?"

"She will bring us, or someone else will," Mr. Shay said. "We've got family coming in town all day."

"Okay, I guess we'll get going then."

Benny opened the door for me, and we both stepped out onto the porch. I looked back as we walked away. Mr. Shay had his arm around Mrs. Shay's shoulders, and she was leaning into him. They were supporting each other. Losing Leigh would change them forever, but I was hopeful they would get through it and be able to continue to live as long as they gave each other strength. I took a deep breath and walked up to Leigh's bug. They'd asked me to drive it to the funeral home so it would be parked out front for the viewing. Mr. Shay had loaded some things from Leigh's room that I asked for into the backseat.

"You okay?" Benny asked when I stopped at the bug.

"Yeah," I nodded. "I'm okay."

I opened the driver's side door and got in the little car. I couldn't help but laugh. My knees were scrunched up because of how close the seat was to the steering wheel. Leigh was not a tall woman. I wasn't exactly tall either, but Leigh was more than a little short at only 5'1" on a good day in shoes. After adjusting the seat, I started up the car and followed Benny out of the driveway. When we got to the funeral home, there were a bunch of cars in the parking lot. As I pulled Leigh's impossible-to-miss car into the entrance of the home, a group of people came outside to watch.

I smiled despite the occasion. So many people had turned out to help. Leigh was really loved and was going to be missed by so many. Kelly and her boyfriend, Mary and her sister, and at least 15 other people, some I knew, some I didn't, were there to help. I got the word out to people from school, from Leigh's old dance class, and from her work that I was looking for some help and memorabilia for the viewing tonight and funeral tomorrow. As I climbed out of the bug, two more cars entered the parking lot. And they didn't come empty-handed. Some were holding toolboxes, others had stacks of pictures, pink ribbons, poster boards, and laptops or iPads.

My cousin Kelly walked up to me and pulled me into a hug.

"I'm so sorry about Leigh, but it is also so good to see you," she said into my ear as she held me in the hug.

"I missed you too," I replied quietly.

I felt others around me as I backed away from Kelly. Looking around, even though I knew how well-liked Leigh was, it still shocked me how many people had turned out. Especially the people that weren't local anymore.

"Hey Jimmy," I said as Leigh's old on-again, off-again boyfriend in high school, Jimmy Moore, came up to me. "I heard you live in Virginia Beach now?"

"Yeah," he said. "Closer to Norfolk, but I'm down that way. I had to be here, though." He shrugged and looked down at his feet.

"I know." What else was there to say? We all had to be there because it was the last thing we could do for someone who had been a great friend. Always ready to help, always ready with a joke when a laugh was needed, or a tissue when all you wanted to do was cry.

Danielle Dade, Carrie Hoffman, Steve Ceratino, Natalie Andrews... as I scanned the crowd, I heard another car door. Turning around, I spotted Jack walking up to us with TJ, Max, and Nick in tow.

Benny came up and put his arm around me. "You okay?" he asked quietly. I nodded because it was all I could do at the moment. I took a deep breath to hold my emotions in check.

"I'm glad so many of you could make it," I started. "Leigh was the best of us. Maybe that's why God picked her so early." Another deep breath. If I couldn't get through talking to everyone here in the parking lot, how would I get through tomorrow?

"I'm not going to pretend to understand why Leigh had to leave us, but I believe she is looking down on us all right now, probably laughing and wondering why we are making such a fuss. I swear I could feel her watching me while I drove her bug here. She'll come back and haunt us all if we get so much as a scratch on her baby," I joked.

Everyone laughed a little. "Maybe we should put velvet ropes around it so people don't get too close," Jimmy said. I think he was only half joking. He knew how much Leigh loved that car.

"Well," I said with a sigh as people got somber again. "Let's get started." We all headed into the funeral home with all the memorabilia and tools we brought.

Later that evening, as I got ready for the viewing, everything we had done that day, all the people that helped, and all the memories that were stirred up, ran through my head. I hoped tonight went well. I wanted Leigh's parents to see a celebration of her life, not a focus on the tragedy of her death. Downstairs Benny, Uncle Rob, and Ruby sat at the kitchen table, drinking coffee and talking. When I walked in, Ruby came over and gave me a hug.

"You okay?" Ruby asked as she eyed me critically, looking for signs that I might break.

"I'm okay."

Uncle Rob put his arm around my shoulders and pulled me to him. "We're here for you kiddo, whatever you need," he said.

I nodded and smiled. I was so glad they were there. I couldn't help comparing this scene with a very similar one years ago when we were getting ready to go to my parents' viewing and memorial. We were all younger and standing in a different kitchen, but Uncle Rob and Ruby were there then too, offering the same love and support. I hadn't appreciated it then. My anger at everything and everyone clouded anything else around me. It blocked any other feelings. But I could appreciate them today. I could feel their love and caring. I finally understood how lucky Benny and I truly were and are. We weren't on our own and never had been.

I wanted to make Leigh's parents feel that way, too. There was no way to replace Leigh and, with her death, there were some things the Shays' had lost and would never get back. But they were loved; they weren't alone; they had friends and family. I sent a silent prayer to heaven and promised Leigh I would stick by her parents and do what I could to help them move forward from here. We made our way out to Uncle Rob's Ford F-150 truck and piled in. The ride to the funeral home was a silent one. We were all lost in our own thoughts. We got there early. I wanted to check things over one more time and be there when everyone started arriving.

I walked around and turned on the various iPads and laptops that were scattered all over. The funeral director started playing The Piano Guys playlist I created over the loudspeakers on low. Just enough to have background noise but not make it hard to have conversations. Benny was out front making sure the spotlight we'd brought shone on Leigh's pink bug. I joined him out front as Jack pulled into the parking lot. TJ and Nick were with him, and Max pulled in right behind him with Mr. and Mrs. Hallowell. Again, that feeling of appreciation for everything I had washed over me. All around me were the most important people in my life. They were what I had been missing for all those years away.

My family.

"Everything looks great, Tessie," Jack said as he walked up to me.

"I think so too. I hope her parents are okay with it," I said.

"I think they will be," he said, looking around. "It really captures who she was."

"Hey Tess," Mrs. Hallowell said as she came over and gave me a hug. As I hugged her, I could see another car pull into the parking lot over her shoulder. It was the Shays. They were with Leigh's aunt. My stomach did a somersault. Nothing was ever going to make this good for them, but I wanted them to feel like their daughter had been properly memorialized. As they walked up to the entrance, they took their time and looked at Leigh's pink bug parked out front with the spotlight on it. As it got darker, it would make the car impossible to miss. There were pink tulips placed on the windshield and pink and black ribbons draped over top of it.

Leigh's mom cried harder at the sight of her daughter's car. She clung to her husband with one hand and a tissue with the other. They stared at Leigh's car and held each other while the rest of us went inside to give them some privacy.

There was a large picture of Leigh at the funeral home entrance. In the picture, she was outside and smiling. It had been taken just as she was turning her head to the camera. Her hair blew in the breeze as the sun went down behind her. There were vases of pink tulips everywhere. It had been a massive effort, but I'm pretty sure we bought every last tulip in Virginia. People brought them from Northern Virginia, from Roanoke, from Virginia Beach. Pink tulips in mason jars with black ribbons tied around them were all over the funeral home.

On the table next to where visitors could sign the register, there was an iPad set up playing The Breakfast Club. The volume was muted but most people had seen that movie so many times sound was not needed. All around the room were collages of Leigh. People had brought all the pictures they had and spent most of the day putting collages together and hanging them up. Birthdays, holidays, weddings, vacations, and random no-occasion-at-all pictures were everywhere you looked. There were pictures of a baby Leigh playing with Christmas wrapping paper, then some of a toddler Leigh at her first dance class, then a preteen in braces making goofy faces at the camera, then a grown-up Leigh on her high school graduation day with an arm around each parent and a big smile.

All around the funeral parlor, in the alcoves, on the shelves, was a laptop or iPad playing a John Hughes movie. One alcove showed a young Molly Ringwald pining for Jake in Sixteen Candles, while a couple feet down on a bookshelf, Matthew Broderick was trying to talk a reluctant Cameron into taking out his father's Ferrari. They all played silently as people made their way to the back of the room to see Leigh one last time.

We covered her casket in pink tulips and draped it with pink and black ribbons. Another big picture of Leigh stood on an easel next to it. The common theme of all her pictures, from baby to adult, was her smile. At the end of the day, Leigh was a happy person. She lightened a room when she entered. As much as she loved watching the angst-filled teenagers in John Hughes movies, she was nothing like them. She had her ups and downs, same as anyone, but she always tried to make the best of things.

She had a good life. That's what I wanted to show her parents. It was cut short. It was unfair, and no one was ever going to make that okay for them, but we could at least show them they had given her a good life while she was here.

People steadily streamed through the doors of the funeral home now. I watched from a corner in the back as the Shays made their way around the room and talked to family and friends. They were doing their best to stay strong and talk to everyone that wanted to offer their condolences. They slowly made their way to Leigh's casket where people backed off and gave them space. Leigh's mom put her hand on her daughter's casket and bowed her head. Her shoulders shook as she cried. Mr. Shay stood next to her, tears falling down his face as he silently cried. I kept my distance. I wanted to be close by if needed, but not hovering and crowding them.

After a few minutes, I glanced back towards them and caught Mr. Shay's eyes. He gestured for me to come over. Taking a deep breath and trying to control my emotions, I walked over to them. Mr. Shay squeezed my shoulder and Mrs. Shay enveloped me in a hug when she saw me.

"Thank you, Tess," she whispered in my ear as we hugged.

"You did a great job," Mr. Shay said as he tried to wipe the tears off his face.

"She was my best friend and like a sister," I said. "I love her. I always will.

# Chapter 14

## THE EULOGY

*"Good-bye may seem forever. Farewell is like the end, but in my heart is the memory and there you will always be."*

— Walt Disney

A s people filed into the church and sat down, I clutched my notes. I was in the second pew right behind Mr. and Mrs. Shay. They quietly held hands and stared at the casket a couple of feet away. *You can do this* was on repeat in my head. I really wanted to go home, crawl into bed, and stay there for about a month. But that was no way to honor Leigh's life. Giving her eulogy was the last thing I could do for her, and I was going to do it well. Hopefully, I could keep it together and not break down.

My heart was breaking watching Leigh's parents, her aunt, her friends and neighbors, everyone that had turned out because Leigh was a person who would be missed terribly. She left a very noticeable gap in the world. The pastor spoke about Leigh growing up and how God could only be apart from some people for a very short while before He had to call them home. He was trying to provide comfort. He did, in a way, but it was a small comfort.

"Leigh's best friend growing up, Tess McCabe, is going to say a few words," the pastor said.

For a second, my breath stopped in my chest, and I froze. Goose bumps broke out over my body, and it felt like every nerve I had stood on end. Then, just as fast as I felt the anxiety attack coming on, it was gone, and a calmness washed over me. I took a deep breath and walked up to the podium at the front of the church.

Standing behind it, I looked down at my notes and made sure I was calm, and my emotions were under control.

The packed church silently stared back at me. Every pew was full, and people were standing in the back. Friends we went to school with from preschool to high school, Benny, Jack and his family, our teachers, our high school principal, coworkers from Leigh's job, and, of course, Leigh's family. Everyone had turned out on this sunny Saturday to pay their respects and lay Leigh to rest.

"Wow, Leigh was so loved in life," I said while I looked around at everyone. It wasn't how I planned to start but, staring into the sea of faces, it was so true.

"Leigh and I met at my grandmother's house when she used to babysit Leigh. At least, that's the earliest memory I have of us together. It seems like we've always known each other. We used to tell everyone we were sisters. When they would point out that we looked absolutely nothing alike, we would just say "so," shrug our shoulders, and run off. Even then, on some level, I think we knew we had a bond that was special. A bond that would see us through wins and losses, first crushes, arguments, bad breakups, and even life-changing events."

I paused and took a deep breath as the memories of my parents' funeral flashed through my head.

"Leigh was the good one," I said, making air quotes and rolling my eyes. "I know most of you think any trouble we got into was my fault." I laughed a little. Some others in the church laughed with me, and even Mrs. Shay gave me a small smile.

"Don't underestimate the brilliance that was Leigh, though. I can take credit for all the things we did that just did not work out as intended. Riding the wagon down the big sledding hill on the Hallowell farm comes to mind. Leigh ended up with a broken arm; I had a knot on my forehead; and I think Jack got grounded for the rest of the summer. Trying to get out and go to the carnival without our parents when we were eleven was another one that didn't go as planned. We didn't make it to the end of the driveway before my mom caught us."

I paused as some more people laughed.

"But Leigh had her moments too. She was just smarter about it than the rest of us. When she came up with something, she thought it through and planned it out. We had a much better chance of success when Leigh was running the show. Most of the time. There's always that one time for everyone when things don't go as planned."

I paused here and took a breath. I could see curiosity on some faces. Jack's mom leaned over and asked Jack what I was talking about. He shrugged. I hoped she didn't ground him again after she heard the story. Jack was a grown man, but I'm pretty sure that would not matter to his mom.

"Okay, so we've kept this secret for over 10 years, but I think we can finally tell the story, as it is too good not to share. We were camping out on my parent's farm. Leigh and I were about twelve, I think. Jack may have just turned thirteen and Benny was maybe fifteen. It was the last weekend of summer before school started and hot as, well, H-E-double hockey sticks as Leigh would say when we were younger."

"Benny was being a moody teenager about having to be out there with us in that heat. My parents told him he had to watch us." I looked at Benny and smiled, and he rolled his eyes at me.

"We were all hot, but it was the last camp out of the season, and no one wanted to go in the house. We were sitting around trying to think of something to do that wouldn't make us hotter than we already were. And it was Leigh who said the words, 'I wish we could go take a dip in the lake.' That sounded like a brilliant idea to four kids sitting around on a swelteringly hot night in August."

"For those who don't know, 'the lake' was a man-made lake the Hallowells had dug out and kept clean on their farm for the boys to swim in when they were kids. We all agreed we should have had the campout at the Hallowells, but it was too late now. It was a good five miles down the road."

"I'm pretty sure it was Benny who pointed out that going through the fields was a much shorter distance. We were discussing the merits of walking there and back again when Leigh mentioned the tractor. Yes friends, keep in mind, this was our Leigh's idea. Not mine. Just want to emphasize that again."

Everyone in the church smiled. I took a deep breath and kept going.

"'What if we take the tractor?' Leigh says. We stopped talking for a second and thought about it and all came to the same conclusion. Leigh was brilliant. Taking the tractor was a great idea. Do I need to tell you now that taking the tractor did not go well?"

More laughter from the pews.

Mr. And Mrs. Shay listened with rapt attention. They had never heard this story before. No one had. That's why I wanted to share it today.

"Those of you who remember my parents' old farm know the barn was actually not very close to the house. We thought it would be far enough away that we could get the tractor out without waking up anyone in the house. And we did. Benny had it up and running and out of the barn in a matter of minutes. The fact that we could probably walk faster than the tractor was going to be able to go carrying all of us didn't occur to us or really matter anymore."

As I told the story, I could see it all happening again, like it was yesterday. Leigh was smiling and laughing while she joked around with everyone. Thinking about her that night, it occurred to me she might have had a small crush on Benny. She wasn't blatantly flirting or anything but, remembering it now, she was very attentive to whatever he had to say. I had never noticed it before, and she had never said anything. She probably knew nothing would ever come of it; it was her own private fantasy she kept to herself. Made me wonder how many other things I never noticed or didn't pay enough attention to. But I guess we all have some private thoughts and feelings we don't share with anyone else.

"We all piled onto the tractor around Benny. Don't ask me how we all fit on there, but we made it work. Benny headed through our field toward the Hallowell's farm. I don't think any of us gave a proper amount of thought to the terrain that we were trying to cut through. As kids, we had run through those fields and knew them like the back of our hand. But, trying to take a tractor across them in the dark, well, that was a different story. I think we would've made it had it not been for all the rain we had earlier that week. A lot of rain. So, we were going through muddy fields and then we get to what is usually a creek. After nearly a week of heavy rain, it was more like a small river."

I glanced at my brother sitting with Jack, TJ, Nick, and Max. He had his head down like he wished he could sink into the pew and disappear. Jack and his brothers chuckled. Benny lifted his head and caught my eye, then smiled, shaking his head at me. He knew I was going to tell this story, but he seemed to have forgotten what a starring role he had in it.

"We were not to be deterred, though," I continued. "And if I remember right, it was Leigh who said we could make it through. After all, we'd crossed that creek a thousand times before on a tractor, she had reasoned. So much in fact that you could see the path where we always crossed in our flashlights' beams that were lighting the way for Benny. The water was just higher, that's all," I said with a roll of my eyes.

"Oh good grief," Mrs. Shay said from the first pew while shaking her head. Mr. Shay smiled through the tears running down his face.

"To my brother's credit, I think he tried to express some misgivings about this idea, but we gave him a wrath of crap about chickening out. Hindsight, being what it is, he may have been right that it wasn't a good idea."

"Might have been right?" Benny said incredulously from the pew.

"I think we can all agree now that it wasn't a good idea, Tess," T.J. chimed in. I saw his mom shoot him a look that could've peeled paint off a car. I hadn't gotten to the part that Jack's brothers played in this story yet. She's now wondering how many of her children were involved in this scheme. The answer - all of them.

"Alright, alright, enough from the peanut gallery," I said as people murmured about the merits of trying to go through with it.

"We annoyed Benny enough that he went against his better judgment and continued on," I said, pausing a moment for dramatic effect. "He probably shouldn't have done that." People were laughing and Mrs. Hallowell looked like she would skin all of her boys - my brother included - alive after the memorial. It didn't matter that this happened over ten years ago, and all the boys were now grown men.

"Needless to say, we got stuck and when I say stuck, I mean we were STUCK GOOD. The front tires of the tractor wouldn't go up the other side of the creek. Benny tried to back up and the wheels just spun in the mud. We all jumped off the tractor and tried to help him by pushing it forward. The front tires just got stuck deeper and wouldn't move. Luckily, it wasn't actually in the creek, it was kind of straddling it. So, the front tires were on one side and the back tires were on the other. By this point, we were all soaking wet and muddy and knew we needed help."

I noticed Jack's brothers in the pews, actively avoiding their mother's gaze at this point of the story.

"So, Jack and Benny ran the rest of the way to the Hallowell's farm and got Jack's brothers," I continued. "Leigh and I waded in the creek and had a great time until they finally got back. They brought an old red wagon filled with two bales of straw. Jack used to pull Leigh and me around in that same wagon when were kids. In fact, it was the same red wagon that we were riding down the hill in when Leigh broke her arm. All of them were hot and sweaty in this heat while Leigh and I were soaking wet and laughing. Looking back, I can see why they may have been slightly annoyed."

That got outright laughter from everyone. Even Jack's mom smiled while she rolled her eyes.

"Leigh got them smiling soon by just being Leigh. She started goofing around and splashing them with water to cool them off. Eventually, we were all splashing each other and dripping in creek water. Leigh was great at making the best of anything. She could make anything fun. That was her gift. One of her gifts, anyway. Once we were all good and drenched, we did something about the stupid tractor. We spread the hay over the mud and stuffed it under the tires. There was a pretty intense debate over whether we should push the tractor forward over the creek and onto the road, where someone might see us and tell our parents, or try to push the tractor back and go through the fields the way we came."

"Leigh was the tiebreaker. Jack, T.J., and I wanted to go back the way we came. Benny, Max, and Nick said we should go forward and take the road back. Leigh, as was her normal style, thought it through and weighed the merits of each option. In the end, she decided that looking at the terrain, we were more likely to move the tractor forward than back, and given the time of night, we were not likely to run into anyone. At least not anyone that would rat us out."

"She was right. Unless you were there, no one here knew this story until today. We got the tractor out and back home. We even had time to rinse it off and put it back in the barn, none the worse for wear. Everyone went back to their own homes and rooms except for Leigh, who came with me and put on clean clothes so that when the parents got up the next morning, we looked clean and innocent. Me having muddy clothes in the laundry was common enough that my mom wouldn't question it."

"So, we got away with it. For over ten years. But, it's a great story. I wanted to share it with everyone here. It had all the elements that made Leigh, Leigh. She was a little daring, very fun-loving, smarter than most, a great goofball, and the very best friend anyone could hope for. In a tight spot, you wanted her on your side. During your darkest days, when you didn't think you would ever find the light again, she would stick by you. She would throw you a rope to lead you out of the darkness and, if you threw the rope back at her, she would just throw it again. And again. And again. She was relentless and would never give up on the people she cared about... even when they had given up on themselves."

"Most of all, Leigh loved life. And she would not want us, any of us, to forget to live because we were grieving for her. Henry Wadsworth Longfellow wrote a poem called "A Psalm of Life," that I think Leigh would want us to remember as we leave here today.

### A Psalm of Life
*Tell me not in mournful numbers,*
*Life is but an empty dream!*
*For the soul is dead that slumbers,*
*And things are not what they seem.*
*Life is real!*
*Life is earnest!*
*And the grave is not its goal;*
*Dust thou are, to dust thou returnest,*
*Was not spoken of the soul.*
*Not enjoyment, and not sorrow,*
*Is our destined end or way;*
*But to act, that each tomorrow*
*Find us farther than today.*
*Art is long, and*

*Time is fleeting,*
*And our hearts, though stout and brave,*
*Still, like muffled drums, are beating*
*Funeral marches to the grave.*
*In the world's broad field of battle,*
*In the bivouac of Life,*
*Be not like dumb, driven cattle!*
*Be a hero in the strife!*
*Trust no Future, howe'er pleasant!*
*Let the dead Past bury its dead!*
*Act, - act in the living Present!*
*Heart within, and God o'erhead!*
*Lives of great men all remind us*
*We can make our lives sublime,*
*And, departing, leave behind us*
*Footprints on the sand of time;*
*Footprints, that perhaps another,*
*Sailing o'er life's solemn main,*
*A forlorn and shipwrecked brother,*
*Seeing, shall take heart again.*
*Let us then be up and doing,*
*With a heart for any fate;*
*Still achieving, still pursuing,*
*Learn to labor and to wait."*

I paused and took a breath at the end of the poem. I hope it affected everyone listening as it did me. To me, it screamed that your life is not over. There is still work to be done. I knew firsthand how easy it is to get lost in your grief and forget to live. I didn't want anyone here, especially Leigh's parents, to go down that same dark road.

"Leigh, I will forever be grateful that you picked me to sit next to and share your crayons with at my grandmother's little round kitchen table all those summers ago when we were both still in pigtails. Every time I try to put some curls in my hair, I will think of you. I will remember our Brat Pack binge girl's nights, tubing on the river, too many campouts to count, Sunday church followed by brownies and movies at Ms. Ruby's, Babysitter Club books, Harry Potter movies, and arguing every Halloween over who we should dress up as."

The room was blurry from the tears streaking down my face. Just then, an image of an annoyed Leigh telling me I was making a wreck of my makeup flashed through my head. I tried to wipe my eyes as I faced her coffin.

"I love you. You were my best friend and sister. Though unfairly short, yours was a life well lived. Please be at peace, my friend."

# Chapter 15

# MOVING FORWARD

*"If you dare nothing, then when the day is over, nothing is all you will have gained."*
— Neil Gaiman, The Graveyard Boys

My fingers tapping at the keyboard on my laptop were the only sounds in the tiny house. Everything else was quiet. I sat in the kitchen putting the final touches on the business plan for Benny's shop and salvage yard. He was meeting with the bank this afternoon about his small business loan and had to present the plan.

Leigh's funeral was a week ago, and it was only two weeks ago that I was living in Arlington. It felt like a lifetime had passed since I had lost my job, packed up my life, and moved back home. Reconnecting with friends and family, preparing for Leigh's funeral, helping Benny with his business plan, and debating taking the offer in New York made the past two weeks feel so much longer.

Two days after Leigh's funeral, I finally called Katrina Lucas about the job offer at Frankie's restaurant in New York. I still wasn't sure what I wanted to do. Being back home, I felt like I was finally starting to really live again and have actual connections with people. But, it was because I had changed my mindset, moving to New York shouldn't change it back. And the job was a hell of an opportunity. If I passed, something like it may never come along again. So, I agreed when Katrina asked me to come see her in Arlington while she was in town. We were scheduled to meet up tomorrow.

Sitting back in the chair, I looked around the tiny kitchen. The fresh light-yellow paint offset light brown, worn wood cabinets above old butcher block counter tops that held my mom's old clay kitchen canisters and pots that were various bright colors and scattered all over. Some women had tons of shoes or jewelry, my mom collected clay—clay pots, clay canisters, clay vases. She always wanted to learn pottery but life got in the way. Kids, a full-time job, running a small farm with dad, all of it didn't leave room for much else in the way of hobbies.

Taking a sip of coffee, I brought my head back to the here and now and focused on what I was doing. I continued to scan through the business plan and make some tweaks here and there. It was good. Benny had great ideas and vision for what he could do with the shop and salvage yard. I hoped the bank would see the vision. I had money saved and could help with some of the expense, but it wasn't enough for everything Benny wanted to do. Uncle Rob kept trying to lower the price of the shop or create a payment plan, but Benny wouldn't hear of it. Uncle Rob counted on that money for part of his retirement. He needed it. If Benny couldn't pay him properly for the business, he'd help Uncle Rob sell it to someone who could.

But the shop belonged with Benny. He'd put nearly as much blood and sweat into it as Uncle Rob. "This has to work. The bank has to approve the loan." I took a deep breath and saved the document.

I stood up to stretch and refresh my coffee when I heard a car coming up the driveway. Benny wouldn't be back yet, and I wasn't expecting anyone, but that didn't stop people from dropping by. It was probably Ms. Ruby. When we were younger, she often came by while she was out running errands, just to check on us or more often to drop something off like some cupcakes she made or once she brought a potted plant that would look "perfect on the porch steps." That poor plant didn't have a chance. Benny gave it water out of pity once in a while when it was looking exceptionally brown and dry. I was still young and lost in my head from losing my parents so caring for a potted plant wasn't happening. One day the poor plant was gone from the steps. I later saw it at Ruby's house. She had nursed it back to life, and it was thriving there.

A glance out the window revealed a dusty Ford truck parking next to my worn-out Toyota. It was Jack. I wondered what he was doing here. We hadn't seen each other since Leigh's memorial though I had been by his house to talk to his mom a couple of times. I enlisted her help to review the business plan and provide any suggestions. She had some great insight, and I was grateful to have her help. But Jack was always out, either working on the farm or his photography.

I opened the kitchen door as he got out of the truck in his normal outfit of worn jeans and an old t-shirt. He'd probably already been working for four or five hours this morning, as evidenced by the dirt he tried to brush off his jeans.

"Hey," he said as he walked up to me.

"Hey, this is a surprise. What brings you around?"

He snagged my coffee from my hand and drank as he entered the house. "Coffee."

Smiling and rolling my eyes, I followed him into the kitchen and topped off the coffee in the cup he'd taken and got another cup for myself.

"Okay, you have coffee" I said. "Now, what else brings you around?"

"Well, I wanted to know when we were going out?" he said casually.

"Out." I repeated, a little taken aback. I know we had talked about seeing where things led when I was at his house for dinner the other night, but we didn't make any plans to go on a date or anything.

"Out," he repeated, taking another sip of his coffee.

"When did we decide we were going out?"

"We said we want to see where whatever is still between us goes. Why wait? What did your dad always say? Shit or get off the pot."

"Charming."

"And true," he shot back.

I got the feeling that there was something he wasn't saying. Something that made this a little more pressing than it had been but he didn't elaborate.

"Come on Tessie, let's seize the carp," he said, looking at me over his cup while he took another sip of coffee. His eyes laughed at his own joke. It was from one of our favorite movies, Out Cold. We'd watched it too many times to count and could probably recite the whole script by heart until the day we died.

"You are quoting a character named Pigpen to get me to go on a date with you," I said.

"And its working," he replied.

I rolled my eyes. "Don't get overconfident." But, I was smiling.

I enjoyed being able to talk like this with him. I had missed it.

I didn't want to lose it.

I leaned against the counter, staring at the floor while my coffee got cold in my hand. Jack patiently sat at the kitchen table drinking his like he didn't have a care in the world and would wait for me to come around to his way of thinking.

"Okay," I said. "One date and we'll see how it goes from there."

"Great, does tomorrow night work?" he asked after he drained the last of his cup, stood and stretched. I admit my insides did a little leap of excitement watching him.

I debated telling him I had a meeting in Arlington tomorrow and seeing if we could wait but then I would have to explain why I had a meeting and with who. For whatever reason, I wasn't ready to talk about the job offer. I wanted to know more before bringing it up to my friends and family. The meeting was in the morning so I should be back in plenty of time to go to dinner, albeit I would probably be a bit tired.

"Where are you taking me? Hot dogs and fries?" I asked teasingly while he washed his cup and put it in the strainer.

"No, I'm a gentleman. Burgers and fries." He winked at me as he finished washing his cup and putting it in the strainer. "I'm still working on where we're going to go. Just be ready around seven."

"Okay."

He reached around me to get the towel off the counter and dry his hands. I looked up at him as he stood in front of me. Slowly, I think to give me a chance to duck and run if I wanted, he leaned in and gave me a soft kiss on the lips. Then another deeper kiss. One of his hands cupped the back of my head and the other was on my waist. My coffee cup was squished between us.

Damn, I really wished I wasn't holding that cup.

"See you tomorrow night," he said, looking into my eyes, then let go of me and walked out the door.

Sitting in the chair he vacated, I stared at my laptop. I didn't need to go on a date with Jack to see how things would go or if I wanted to take our relationship beyond friendship. I already knew. It had always been Jack for me. I don't think I ever stopped loving him truly. The feelings may have gone dormant all those years ago but the second I looked in my rear-view mirror the other week and saw him in his truck behind me, they came alive again.

But I couldn't help wondering if he needed the date to know if he wanted to move forward with me? I sensed there was something he wasn't saying. Did he really wake up this morning and decide today was the day to figure this out? I had been gone a long time, and we didn't end things well last time. The circumstances were different but still; it was ugly. Jack said he hasn't really connected with anyone since then except maybe that grad student who'd moved to Colorado, but that didn't necessarily mean he was ready to go back down that road with me again either.

"Stop," I mumbled to myself. "You will drive yourself crazy thinking about this."

Refocusing my attention back onto the business plan, I read through it again for the millionth time and saved it to a thumb drive. Benny still had the same black and white printer that he bought for me when I was in high school. The thing probably had cobwebs in it from lack of use. I wanted his business plan to be printed in color on good quality paper which I couldn't do here.

I cleaned my coffee cup, hit the bathroom, and was out the door within a few minutes. I headed to Ms. Ruby's house to use her printer, and then we had plans to have lunch with Mrs. Shay. The Shays were doing as well as could be expected, I supposed. They were trying to go back to work and get back into a routine, but it was going to take time. I stopped by there on Wednesday evening and the lights were out and the doors locked up tight. It was 6 o'clock and still light outside. Mrs. Shay normally would've had the front door open so a breeze could come in through the screen. More often than not she would sit on the porch with a glass of wine talking on the phone with her sister or chatting with neighbors.

It was weird to see the house closed up tight and dark. Their cars were in the carport, so I knew they were home. I called Ruby and told her we had to do something, so she called Mrs. Shay the next day and talked her into having lunch.

The funeral was over. We had laid Leigh to rest. And life kept going. People went back home, back to work, no one forgot Leigh, but they had lives to get back to. It was natural. For me, watching everyone else carry on with their lives had been the hardest part after losing my parents. I felt like my world had stopped, and I didn't know how to start it back up again. Even worse, I wasn't sure I really wanted to. I imagined the Shays were feeling the same way. But Leigh wouldn't want them to spend the rest of their lives in mourning. She would want them to find happiness again. It was going to take time, but we had to start somewhere.

I pulled into Ruby's drive and parked. She was out front watering her flowers and looked a bit more like her old self. She wore a huge, bright pink woven sun hat that could probably provide shade for a few people, a black shirt with different colored triangles all over it, and a long, flowing green skirt. Her sandals were dark brown with straps covered in multi-colored beads. This was the Ruby I remembered from my childhood.

She waved as I got out of the car. She had on make-up and had pulled her hair back into a smart chignon at the base of her neck.

"Hey honey," she said as I came up the walk.

"Hey, can I go in and use your printer real quick before we go?" I held up the thumb drive.

"Absolutely. I've been praying for Benny. I hope this goes his way. He's worked so hard all his life. I want him to have this."

"Me too." I entered the house, which hadn't changed that much, though you could see some wear and tear. I guess it would've been hard for her to keep up with things when she was so sick; but there were paint swatches on the table, so I had a feeling paint rollers were in my near future.

*If I was still around.* The thought drifted through my head, but I put it aside. I had a long drive tomorrow, plenty of time to contemplate my future then.

I went onto the little enclosed back porch where Ruby kept her office and stuck the thumb drive in her laptop. After I got the business plan printing, I looked around the small room. There were old pictures hanging on the walls. There was one of Ruby holding me when I was a baby sitting next to my mom with little Benny squeezed in between them. I imagined it was my dad holding the camera for that picture. There was another picture of an older Benny and me eating ice cream outside on Ruby's back steps. You could watch Benny and me grow up and my parents get older from the pictures on Ruby's wall. Turning back to the laptop, I picked up the picture that had sat on Ruby's desk for as long as I could remember. It was one of the few family portraits we had done professionally when I was growing up. I was maybe 10, Benny would've been about 13, and Dad had hired a photographer to come to the house and do a family portrait. Mom had decorated a small spruce tree in front of our house with Christmas lights and a bright star. Benny and I sat on a straw bale that was covered in a red plaid blanket while Mom and Dad stood on either side of us with the tree in the background.

I picked up the picture and could feel the familiar ache in my chest that I still got when I thought about my parents and our family the way it once was. The ache wasn't constant anymore like it was when I was younger, but it would still come around now and then. I had a feeling it always would. But now I had learned how to acknowledge it and then move on with the business of living so it would fade away again until some other thought or memory brought it back.

The printer stopped, and I set the picture back down on the desk. I heard Ruby come back in the house and I went back out into the kitchen to meet her.

"You look great. Is that a new outfit?" I asked.

"Oh, no, I've had this for a while but haven't worn it in some time," she replied. "I have good news. I just got offered a full-time position at the high school next year teaching senior biology. I cannot wait! Lunch is on me today."

"That's great Ruby! I'm so happy for you." I pulled her into a big hug. This was a big step toward getting her life back. While being so happy for Ruby, I wasn't sure how much Mrs. Shay would feel like celebrating anything.

Ruby knew what I was thinking. She pulled back from my bear hug and looked me in the eye.

"We have to start somewhere with getting her to remember to live. I'm not even going to pretend to imagine what she's going through.

There is nothing worse in the world than losing a child, but Leigh would want us to make sure her parents are okay. So, that's what we're going to do."

"You're right. I wish I knew better how to do that, but whatever it takes, we'll help them through this."

"You got your printouts? Are you ready to go?"

"Yes." I held up the business plan. I had made multiple copies, figuring Benny would need more than one at the bank. "Can we swing by the shop so I can drop these off to Benny?"

"Of course, of course, let's roll," she said, grabbing her keys.

We pulled up in front of the Shay's house and parked. Uncle Rob's truck was in the driveway. He wasn't at the shop when we dropped the business plan off to Benny. Apparently, he'd been here for a while, according to Benny.

"I didn't know that Uncle Rob and the Shays were that close of friends."

"Well, Rob and Patrick were best friends in high school," Ruby said absently while digging through her purse.

God only knew what she was looking for. The purse was the size of a small suitcase. All of her purses, and she had a fair number, were like that. When I was a kid, I thought she was Mary Poppins. Anything you could want, Ruby could pull out of her purse.

"They were?! How did I not know that for all these years? You never see them together."

"Well, it's a long story and happened a long time ago. Truthfully, it's not my story to tell, but it is a good one," Ruby said wistfully. It was killing her not to tell me. "Let's just say there is one thing that will ruin a lifelong friendship every time." She gave me a "you know what I'm talking about" look.

I thought for a second. "They liked the same girl?"

"Oh, they more than liked. They were both head over heels in love with her. The little trollop," Ruby said.

"Wow." I was truly shocked. For one, Ruby never talked bad about anyone, so this girl must have really done a number to have Ruby call her something like that. Two, I guess I was still child-like in how I thought of my family and couldn't imagine Mr. Shay or Uncle Rob in high school going after the same girl.

And three, "Who says trollop anymore Ruby?" I said jokingly as I got out of the car.

Mrs. Shay opened the screen door before Ruby could reply. "Hi Ruby, hey Tess, come in," she said.

It seemed like she was trying to seem happier than she actually was, but I would take it. Sometimes, you had to fake it until you make it. But that would only get her so far. She would need friends, family, and maybe even therapy for the rest. Today was a small first step to moving, not so much on, as forward.

Uncle Rob and Mr. Shay sat at the kitchen table drinking coffee and laughing over something as we walked in. Despite the laughing, I could tell Mr. Shay had also been crying. His eyes were red and slightly bloodshot. That he hadn't been getting much sleep lately was a safe assumption.

"Hey Uncle Rob," I said, leaning over and giving him a quick hug. "What are you guys up to?"

"Oh, just trying out this retirement thing," Uncle Rob said. "I'm heading to the shop a little later to cover things while Benny's at the bank. Is he all set with the business plan?"

"Yes, we just came from there. I dropped off seven copies."

"Rob was just telling us about some of his ideas for growing the shop and getting the salvage yard," Mr. Shay said. "It's a big undertaking. Let Benny know if he needs any advice from an accounting standpoint to call me. I'm happy to help him out."

"Actually, that would probably be great," I said. "I think he's been so focused on getting the funding for everything he wants to do, I don't know if he's thought about how to handle it all when he actually gets the money and needs to put it to work."

"Patrick would be a good person for him to talk to," Uncle Rob agreed, nodding his head. "I'll talk to Benny about it."

Ruby touched my arm and sent me a look. She nodded her head over toward the front door. I looked over to see Mrs. Shay standing by the coat rack. She was staring at a simple pink purse hanging there. Leigh's purse. My heart caught in my throat as a wave of grief rushed over me, but I took a breath and squelched it. Me breaking down would help no one, least of all Mrs. Shay, who looked so lost.

Ruby walked over and put an arm around her shoulder. "You ready to go to lunch, honey?" she asked quietly.

Mrs. Shay took a deep breath and nodded. Her hair was a bit of a mess and she didn't have on any makeup. Were we pushing her to go out too soon? Maybe we should give her more time?

"Patrick, Rob, do you want us to bring you back anything?" Ruby asked.

"No, I think we're good," Mr. Shay said. "Becca made us some eggs and bacon earlier."

Ruby nodded and turned back to Mrs. Shay, gently nudging her towards the door. She moved quietly out the door without looking back.

Later that afternoon, I pulled into a parking space outside of Uncle Rob's—hopefully soon to be Benny's—shop. I cut off the engine but let the keys hang there for a minute and laid my head back in the seat. I finally let a few of the tears I'd been holding back all afternoon fall. Mrs. Shay had been quiet for most of the lunch. She congratulated Ruby on her new teaching position and offered to help with the shop, but she mostly just listened while Ruby and I did all the talking.

"It was a start, Leigh," I whispered. "We'll get them through this. Don't worry."

Drying my eyes quickly with the back of my hands and grabbing the keys, I got out of my car and headed into the shop. There were a couple of people in the waiting room watching television. One guy stood staring at the vending machine but didn't seem to find anything that interested him and sat back down to stare at his phone.

I went around the counter to go back into the garage. Benny really needed to have someone working the counter full-time instead of people sitting in the waiting room for him or Uncle Rob to come out of the garage.

Benny was digging through a toolbox at the far end of the garage while Uncle Rob talked to one of the other part-time mechanics.

I walked as quick as could without breaking into a run over to Benny. "Well?!"

He sighed and looked down at the floor. For a second, my heart stopped. Then he broke out into a big smile. "I got the loan."

I smiled back and grabbed him into a hug.

Shit just got real.

# Chapter 16

# TURNING POINT

*"So be sure when you step, Step with care and great
tact. And remember that life's A Great Balancing Act.
And will you succeed? Yes! You will, indeed! (98 and ¾
percent guaranteed) Kid, you'll move mountains."*
— Dr. Seuss, Oh, The Places You'll Go!

Passing yet another tractor trailer driving down I-81 on my way
back to Arlington, it occurred to me it was three weeks to the day
since I got fired, heard about Leigh's death, and came back home. It
felt like so much more time had passed. I think I experienced life and
emotions and really being with people more in the last three weeks
than I had in the eight years since my parents died.

Normally I would play music, an audiobook, or a podcast while
driving. Anything to not only pass the time but also make it so I
don't have to think about anything. But not today. Today, I was going

to use this long drive as an opportunity to really figure out what I wanted to do and where I wanted to do it. The car was quiet as I sped down the highway, cutting through green valleys and mountains in the background.

Memories of the past two weeks, of my childhood, of my family and friends, swirled in my head and mingled with memories of working at the The Olive Tree and how much I loved it. I let myself think about New York and the possibilities of starting somewhere new and how scary exciting that could be. By the time I finally arrived in Arlington, I hadn't made any final decisions, but I knew better what I was prioritizing and what I was letting go.

Ready to talk to Katrina, I pulled into a parking spot and walked into the coffee shop where we were meeting. I was pleasantly surprised to see it was actually quiet and not packed full of people looking for their mid-morning cup of caffeine fix. Though I was early, I was surprised to see Katrina was already sitting at a table tucked away in the corner so we could have some privacy.

I approached her table. "Katrina? Hi, I'm Tess McCabe," I said in case she didn't remember what I looked like.

"Yes, Tess, it's great to see you again. Please have a seat."

"Thanks."

As I sat down, I noticed she had sample menus scattered in front of her.

"I'm reviewing different options for the menu. Trying to determine what will fit for New York City. Any thoughts?" she asked as she handed me some of the menu samples to look at.

I looked through the menus. The dishes were not what you would see on a dinner menu at The Olive Tree. These were high-end, fine-dining style dishes. The meals were no less than six courses.

"Frankie's is fine dining?"

"Well, we are rolling out something new and thought what better place to start than New York City. This isn't a typical Frankie's but we are trying to keep that hush hush. We will be Francesco's," she said with a smile. "It will have the food and service of a fine-dining establishment without the stuffy atmosphere."

Katarina's excitement for the project was apparent. I could tell she really believed in it and had a vision in her head that she was trying to create.

"Sounds exciting. Are you having fun getting it all off the ground?"

"I am loving it. This is one of my favorite projects yet. Plus, I love New York. Always have," Katrina replied. Her enthusiasm for both the project and New York were apparent.

"I've only ever been once as a kid with my family." Happy memories surfaced in my head. My dad walking with me on his shoulders to keep from getting trampled by the crowds in Times Square. My mom asked Benny to hold her hand, so she didn't get swept away by all the people. If Benny saw through this ruse, he didn't say it. He played along and held her hand like she wanted. Thinking back now, I realized he may have been overwhelmed by all the people too and as worried as my mom was that he would get separated from us.

"Have you considered what it would be like to move there?" Katrina asked.

"I've been thinking about that and the job ever since I talked to Vito. It would be a complete lifestyle change, that's for sure."

Katrina piled the sample menus together, clasping her hands on the top of the pile, and looked at me earnestly. "Let's get down to it Tess. I know the work you did at The Olive Tree. I have the highest respect for Vito and trust his judgement plus I saw for myself everything you did there."

"What about Cass?" I asked. I didn't want to bring up my firing but I also didn't want her to hear about it some other way.

"Ugh, that blow hole. God, I never could stand him and believe me that won't change. I'm aware of what happened. Vito filled me in when I talked to him."

I nodded. That was a relief. I didn't feel like rehashing the whole incident. I could live happily never having to think about or even say the name Cass again. My firing was unjustified and it wasn't just me that thought so.

"Cass is an idiot," Katrina continued. "I don't know what his deal is when it comes to you."

"I'm not sure. I know when Vito hired me and then started putting me in charge and teaching me to be his assistant manager, Cass did not like it. He said I was too young and inexperienced. Vito wouldn't budge though. He argued that I was doing good work and asked how I was supposed to get experience if no one gave me a chance. It was one of the few times I heard Vito really argue with Cass and refuse to go along with what his brother wanted."

"Cass is a petty man. I've known both him and Vito for years. Cass always gets his way. Always. He will be patient and never quit trying until he finds a way, no matter how long it takes."

"Well, I guess he finally got his way then," I said with some bitterness. I loved my work at The Olive Tree and for it all to end in such an ugly way was hard to swallow.

"I am sorry about Cass. But I do believe things happen for a reason," Katrina said. "Let me tell you more about the vision for Francesco's, the role I need you to fill now and where it could go in the future, and then you can ask me any questions you have. Sound good?"

"Sounds perfect," I said.

Katrina spent the next hour going over all the plans for the new restaurant and helping me to see the vision of what Francesco's was to be. She provided a clear picture of what was needed from me, how my performance would be measured, and how my role could change and grow down the road.

"So, what are you thinking?" she asked after she was done.

I sat back in my chair and sighed. Katrina really was dropping an amazing opportunity in my lap. I was young and single with nothing tying me down. If I was going to make a life changing move, this was the time to do it. But, just because this opportunity was presented to me on a silver platter didn't mean it was my only option.

"When would you need me to be in New York?" I asked.

"Honestly, I needed you yesterday. Frankie's can pay for a hotel room for up to three months. That way you don't have to rush to sign a lease somewhere, but I would need you as soon as possible. As early as next week if you can make it happen."

Katrina's cell phone rang, and she excused herself to take the call outside.

I was grateful for the reprieve. I couldn't keep stringing her along. I needed to decide. Logically, it made sense. It was a great move for my career. A new beginning. This wasn't like before. I wouldn't be running away from my family, friends, and home. I would be moving away but keeping them in my life. I knew they would all be supportive.

I tried to picture a life in New York City but other thoughts kept intruding.

Lunch with Ruby and Mrs. Shay.

Having coffee in the shop with Uncle Rob and Benny.

Sitting on the front porch swing with Benny.

Running in the Hallowell's field and drinking coffee with Jack on the tailgate of his truck.

Katrina came back in and sat down at the table. She looked at me for a moment and sighed.

"I really need to know one or another by the end of the week. If you are in, then I need you to be in 100 percent."

"I understand," I said with a nod. "Trust me, if I take the job, I will be fully committed."

She got her stuff together and stood up from the table. "I look forward to your call," she said.

I stood up and shook her hand. "Thank you for taking the time to meet with me and for making such an amazing offer. I will let you know my decision no later than the end of this week."

I sat back down at the table as Katrina made her way out of the coffee shop. Spinning my empty coffee cup in my hand, I debated what to do next. It was nearly lunch time and I hadn't eaten. I should probably have something before heading back.

I was three blocks from The Olive Tree.

It broke my heart that I was nervous about stopping in to see everyone. That restaurant was more than a job to me. It had felt like home for more than two years. I finally started to care about things again while I was working there. I was connecting with people again. I could feel parts of the old Tess -- the Tess before my parents died – surfacing more and more every day. And then it was all ripped away so quickly and hearing about Leigh's death the very same night as being fired had left me reeling.

I had left everyone and everything I had known for the last two years. I had packed all my belongings in the middle of the night and drove out of town. Again.

With a groan, I put my head in my hands and stared down at the table. This was not going to be the pattern for the rest of my life, things get tough and Tess runs away. At least it didn't take me years to come back this time. Even though I was not coming back to Arlington to live, I would stay in touch with the friends I had made and visit the restaurant I loved. Cass would not take that from me.

I got up and left the coffee shop and began walking the three blocks to The Olive Tree.

# Chapter 17

# DIRECTION

*"I may not have gone where I intended to go, but I think
I have ended up where I needed to be."*
— Douglas Adams, The Long Dark Tea-Time of the Soul

S pring was coming to Arlington. The sun was warming my face as I navigated the crowded sidewalks and, maybe for the first time, I actually appreciated the vitality. I had somehow ended up in Arlington after college, but it wasn't due to some grand plan I had for my life. Everyone was applying for jobs in Northern Virginia during senior year, so without giving it much thought, I did too. Vito asked me to come in for an interview and, when I accepted his job offer, he kindly helped me find an apartment as I didn't know the area. The next thing I knew, I was living and working in Arlington.

I was drifting without giving my life much guidance or thought. Before I knew it, two years had passed. Cass firing me was like hitting a brick wall. Leigh's death gave me direction for the immediate future but not the long term. For that, I really had to finally take stock and decide what I wanted from my life. After being at home for a couple of weeks, I felt what it was like to really connect with people again and have something more than just a working relationship. Even Vito, who I was probably the closest with in Arlington, I kept at a distance. It was no way to live. And it wasn't what my parents would've wanted for me. It was time for me to direct my own life, so when the bad things did happen – as there will always be bad things – I could handle it without making drastic life changes like dropping everything and everyone and running away.

With all of these thoughts jumbling around in my head, I made my way through the rush of people trying to enjoy some early spring during their lunch break. Finally reaching the end of the block, I turned the corner and saw The Olive Tree. My nervousness disappeared and was replaced with actual happiness. I looked forward to seeing my coworkers. I had missed them. Pulling open the heavy door, I needed to give my eyes a minute to adjust to the dim interior lighting. Before I could really see who it was, I felt arms wrapped around me in a hug.

"Tess! You're back!" Kayla, one of the hostesses, screeched in my ear.

"Hey Kayla," I said with a laugh. "How are you doing?"

"I'm good now. It took forever to get better from the flu but I'm finally feeling like myself again."

"That's good to hear, I'm glad you are feeling better. I'm in town for a bit this morning and wanted to stop in and say hi. I left pretty quickly and didn't tell anyone goodbye."

Kayla scowled. "Who can blame you after what that jackass Cass did?!"

"So, does everyone know what happened?" I asked.

"Yes, when everyone got over the flu and finally got back to work, Vito had an all hands meeting and told us."

I nodded but didn't say anything. What had he told them? Clearly, he had said that Cass was involved.

As if she could read my mind, Kayla broke into my thoughts.

"I'm sure there must be more to it than what Vito told us but he really didn't hold back. He told us Cass had it in for you. Despite all of your hard work keeping everything going while half of us were out sick, Cass latched onto the month's profits being slightly down and used it as an opportunity to let you go. He even told us that it was a matter of a couple of hundred dollars difference from how we performed the previous month. Without you here, we would've had to close the doors entirely and there would have been no profit."

Kayla slammed the menus down that she had been wiping down and straightening while she talked. "It's not right," she said.

I sighed and smiled. I didn't need affirmation from everyone else to know that I didn't deserve what Cass did to me. But it was nice to know my co-workers were on my side.

"Thanks for having my back Kayla. As long as my friends here believe in me and know I did everything I possibly could, then I can live with that."

"There was never any doubt," Kayla said sincerely.

"Thank you," I said as I gave her another hug. "Everyone in the kitchen?"

"Yes, getting ready to open. Go on back."

I smiled at her and then headed to the kitchen.

The aroma hit me first as I slowly peeked through the swinging kitchen door. The smell of Italian food cooking had to be the best smell in the world. I'm sure there are people that would disagree but garlic and onions sauteing in olive oil and tomatoes being crushed and added to the mix with a little red wine. There was nothing better. Except if you add fresh baking bread.

My stomach growled but luckily a restaurant kitchen isn't the quietest place in the world, so no one heard it.

"Hey Vito, we're going to need to order more tomatoes man, it's getting low," I heard Luis yell from the back of the kitchen.

"I hear ya, I'm going to take care of it," Vito replied. Maybe it was my imagination be he sounded a bit off. Not like his normal good natured self.

I was standing in the doorway taking everything in when Luis came back to the front of the kitchen and spotted me.

"Tess!" he said in his loudest Luis voice and ran over and gave me a hug. "I have missed you!"

"Hey Luis," I replied and returned his hug. "I missed you too."

"I'm sorry about what happened," he said a bit more quietly. "Cass is a dick. There is no other word for him. Honestly, it's made me question if I want to keep working here if something like that can happen."

I didn't get to reply because Vito came up to us then and the servers working today said hi and gave me hugs or squeezed my hand as they went out front to the dining room.

"Hey Vito, I know you guys are getting ready to open, I won't stay long. I just wanted to say hi to everyone since I was in town."

"I'm going to get back to it. It's great to see you," Luis said as he gave me another quick hug so he could get back to chopping, sauteing, and essentially making magic in the kitchen.

"Tomatoes," he said to Vito as he walked away.

Vito rolled his eyes at me. "I know, I know."

I grinned. Luis loved to get under Vito's skin, in a good-natured way. He said it was good for him and kept "the boss man" on his toes.

"It is good to see you," Vito said. "I can't tell you how much we've missed you here."

I had to say, not that I wanted the restaurant to suffer or things to be hard on Vito and the staff, but it did feel good to hear that my work made a difference and was missed.

"I've missed being here," I said. "This place was a huge part of my life." I shrugged. "Maybe too big a part of my life."

Vito nodded. "Maybe it was."

He knew how much I worked better than anyone. I came in on my days off just to check on things. I was always volunteering to cover shifts if someone wanted off.

"As much as it hurt, still hurts, Cass firing me may have done me a favor," I said. "I'm really thinking about my life now, what I want to do, where I want to do it. I'm going to be okay."

"I never had any doubt you would be okay Tess," Vito said. "You are great at what you do but it shouldn't be all you do. If this happening helped you take stock and get some direction for your life, then that is the best thing I could've hoped for."

"Thanks for recommending me to Katrina. I just met with her this morning, and we talked for over an hour about the opportunity and moving to New York."

"So, are you going to take the job?"

"I have until the end of the week to let her know," I replied.

"Whatever you decide, remember what you learned about yourself these past few weeks. Don't go back to focusing only on work and keep people at arm's length."

"I forgot you minored in psychology," I said wryly.

"Ha, I manage a restaurant, a psychology degree would come in handy."

I grinned. "True words my friend."

We could hear the murmuring of voices as the lunch crowd began to come in.

"That's my cue," I said.

"Hey, remember, you have friends here too. Keep in touch," Vito said. He held his pinky out.

"I swear," I said linking my pinky with his. "Tell Amelia and the girls I said hi."

"I will and next time you come to town, we all will have dinner," he said. "If it makes you feel better, my wife has been giving Cass no end of hell for what he did to you. She never liked him that much and this did not improve things."

"Oh no Vito, I don't want things to be bad for your family," I said. This was sincere. Vito had enough stress to deal with at work. I didn't want family issues to be added to it.

He shrugged. "Cass brought this on himself. He can deal with the consequences. Dinner, next time, with Amelia, the girls and me."

"Sounds amazing," I said as I started walking through the swinging kitchen door. "Ciao."

"Ciao amico mio," Vito said as the door swung shut behind me.

# Chapter 18

# SWEET PARTINGS

*"Though nobody can go back and make a new beginni ng... Anyone can start over and make a new ending."*
— Chico Xavier

I stared at my reflection in the mirror. This was the sixth outfit I'd tried on. I didn't remember going through this when I was a teenager going on my first date with Jack. Back then, he took me to the county fair and won me a green stuffed frog that was still hanging off the back of my bed to this day. It wore a t-shirt that said he was "Froggy for Me." I stared at the frog reflected in the mirror behind me and sighed.

Jack tossed the last baseball straight into the opening of the plastic bottle that looked like an antique metal milk jug.

"Nice shot, my friend," said the carnival game worker to Jack. "What would you like?"

Jack looked at me.

"Nope, you won it, you pick it," I said.

"The frog please." He pointed up at the small green stuffed animal.

The man handed it to him. Jack turned to me and said "I'm froggy for you," in an unusually good mimicry of Kermit the Frog.

I smiled and picked up the frog off my bed. Life was so much simpler then. The memory helped calm my nerves and brought a smile to my face. I stared at my outfit, a long spaghetti-strapped maxi dress with tan high-heeled boots. My hair was down, and I had light makeup on. I didn't want to look like I was trying too hard.

He did not need to know that I've been getting ready since four and changed half a dozen times. When Jack and I dated in our teens, it just seemed to happen naturally. We didn't think about should we or shouldn't we. I don't even remember us worrying about what we would do if it didn't work out.

We wanted to date, so we did.

The telltale sound of tires going over gravel came through the open window in my bedroom. Looking outside, I saw Jack's truck coming up the drive.

I sprayed some extra deodorant under my arms and some perfume in the air and did a quick turn through it like my mom had taught me. Grabbing my purse and my phone, I ran down the stairs and out onto the porch as Jack came to a stop outside the house. He swung the driver's side door open and stepped out. He was wearing black boots and jeans with a gray button-down shirt that was untucked with the sleeves rolled up. His hair, which was usually unruly and finger-combed on a good day, was still wet from the shower and looked like he actually tried to brush it.

I watched him walk up to the porch until he came to a stop at the bottom of the stairs

"You look great," he said.

I stepped down until I was on the step above him. Touching the curls at the end of his hair, I responded, "so, do you."

The quip about how he must've borrowed a brush from one of his brothers died on my tongue at the earnest look on his face. I realized I wasn't the only one putting a lot of pressure on this date.

"Ready to go?" he asked.

"As ready as I'll ever be."

Inside the truck, he shifted into reverse but then hit the brake instead of the gas when I touched his arm.

"Is it me, or are we both stressing about this date?" I asked.

He gave me a small grin. Sitting back against the headrest, he dropped his hand off the gearshift and stared up at the truck ceiling. "Yeah, we probably are."

"What do you have planned for us?" I asked.

"I have reservations at Mickey's Grill House."

"That sounds great! But, how about we pretend we're just having beer and subs in my kitchen again?"

"Is that what you would prefer?"

"Ha, over going to Mickey's, not likely. But I want us to relax and enjoy it. This is just you and me; we're going to hang out, have some dinner, maybe a couple of drinks, and have a good time like we always do."

Jack nodded. "It does sound awesome."

I nodded, already a little more relaxed than a few minutes ago. Somehow, knowing he had the same anxiety made me feel better.

"What did you do today?" he asked as he turned the truck around.

"Well, I spent some time at the shop with Benny and Uncle Rob. I worked at the counter for a while to help them out. They are slammed. It was pretty much trial by fire as they really had no time to give me the crash course."

"That's cool. I heard Benny got the loan. Tara told T.J. yesterday when he stopped by the bank."

I rolled my eyes. "Of course, she did. I bet she's going to want to come sniffing around Benny now that he owns a business. Like to see her father tell her that Benny isn't good enough for her now."

"Relax, Benny's a smart guy," he said. "He's not going to fall for that chick again."

"She stomped on his heart last time. Not just stomped; she danced around on it until it was ground into the dirt. I dare her to bring her ass back around."

Jack just smiled.

"What?"

"Nothing, just thinking of telling her she should stop in the shop and say hi. I want to see the show when she runs into you," he joked.

"Shut up."

"Last I heard, she was dating the bank manager or something," he said. "I don't think you have to worry about her going after Benny."

"Good, I don't care who she dates as long as she stays away from him."

"You know they dated a long time ago when they were both in high school. She was even before Alexis," he said rationally.

"And?!"

"Nothing, nothing at all," he said and tried to hide his grin.

"And, please do not bring up Lexie," I said quietly.

The smile slid off his face. He looked like he was about to say something but decided against it. As I preferred to let the subject of Lexie Blake drop, I didn't push him.

We were entering the Harrisonburg city limits, and I stared out the window as the houses became more plentiful and closer together, more stores and office buildings lined the road, and eventually the buildings and stadium for JMU were going by the window.

When I was a kid, I remember always being excited to "go to town" to shop with Mom or have lunch with Dad or dinner out with them both.

It was a treat.

Then I moved to Arlington and the sheer density of the buildings, houses, and people was absolutely suffocating. I would drive west some days just to get away from it all. I would go to The Plains and have lunch or walk around Middleburg or go for a hike in Leopold's Reserve in Haymarket. But I never went further west than that. I never went back home. Not until Leigh's death.

Jack pulled into the restaurant parking lot, and I snapped out of my reverie.

"Ready?" he asked reaching for the door handle.

"Yep," I replied as he got out of the truck.

He walked around the truck and opened my door like I knew he would. As I got out, he held my hand.

We walked into the restaurant and almost ran over the owner, Leo, as he hurried by us. Though he was clearly busy during the dinner rush, he stopped to talk.

"Jack, good to see you," he said, shaking Jack's hand. "Tess, hi honey, I heard you were back. I'm so glad."

"Hey Leo," I said giving him a quick hug. "How have you been?"

"Overall, pretty good. The restaurant is doing well, and Katie and I just got our third grandchild last month," he said with a big smile. "Another girl. If I ever get a grandson, he's going to have a time growing up with all those girls to keep him in line," he said with a big laugh at his own joke.

"That's great, congratulations!" I said and gave him a hug. A big man, he had to stoop to wrap his big arms around me.

"Mom visited Grace last week and said baby Emma is beautiful," Jack added.

The old restaurant owner beamed at the praise of his grand-daughter. When he smiled, the years melted off his face and glimpses of how he looked when he was younger peaked through.

Leo was always so good to my family while I was growing up. Leo tried to source as much food as possible for his restaurant from local farmers. He'd been doing business with Jack's family for as long as I could remember, and he was starting to do some business with my parents' farm just before the car accident. Business from him and some other local restaurants was part of the reason my parents had taken out the loan to expand the farm.

After the accident, when it was just Benny and me, I'd come home from school and find a lasagna or chicken parmesan or big bowl of meatball spaghetti sitting in a cooler on our porch. There was never a note telling us who dropped it off, but we knew the taste of Leo's cooking and probably his wife Katie did the dropping off. Benny would return the cooler to their house, leaving it on their porch in the early morning before he drove to work. A couple of days later, the same cooler, filled with food, would be back on our porch.

It may be due to Leo's influence that The Olive Garden always felt like home to me.

"Let me show you to your table," Leo said, snapping me out of my thought. He gathered some menus and led us through the rustic looking dining area to a booth in the back with some privacy. A candle burned on the table and wall sconces provided the primary lighting around the room.

Leo handed us the menus and told us to get him if we needed anything. He told our server to bring out a bottle of red wine on him.

"Leo, you don't need to do that," Jack protested.

"This is a small gift from me to you," Leo said. "It's best to accept generosity when it's given."

"Thank you, Leo," Jack said, giving in.

"We appreciate it," I said, reaching for his large hand and giving it a squeeze.

"You are both welcome. You kids enjoy your dinner."

Leo headed back to the kitchen as our server brought out the wine and some bread.

After he poured the wine, the server stepped away to give us a few minutes to read the menu. Leo's menu was always changing. He would only serve maybe five or six meals at a time that would be based on the food that was in season and he could source locally.

"What do you think?" Jack asked as he perused the menu.

"I'm leaning towards the beef tenderloin in a white wine sauce with noodles and asparagus," I said. "What about you?"

"That one does sound good," he said, "but I think I'm going to do the pork chops. You ready?"

After the server took our order, I sat back in the booth and sipped my wine while looking around the room. It hadn't changed. Same wooden floor polished so much you could see the light from the wall sconces bouncing off it and making it shine brilliantly. Some nice pictures hung on the walls, and family photos decorated the wooden mantle above the enormous stone fireplace.

"So, you're working the counter at Benny's shop?" Jack asked.

"I'm helping out for now," I hedged. "I'm working on getting an ad on some different hiring sites for him."

"That's good. But, what about your job in Arlington? When do you have to go back?"

I chuckled. "You know, I've been here for three weeks, and you are the first person to ask me that question. Not even Benny has asked me about work."

"Maybe he figured if you wanted to talk about it, you would."

I shrugged. "Yeah, maybe."

Sighing, I took a sip of my wine. I might as well tell someone.

"I got fired. The same day I found out about Leigh."

"Wow, that was a crappy freaking day," Jack said.

"It really was," I said and nodded in agreement. I told him the condensed, cliff notes version of the events that led to the end of my employment at The Olive Tree. I tried not to let it show how much it was a punch to the gut to me still. But Jack was one of my oldest friends and he knew it hurt me.

"I'm sorry Tessie. That is so frustrating and, at the risk of sounding childish, it is so unfair." He reached across the table and held my hand. "And then to find out about Leigh right afterwards is truly horrible."

"Thanks, talking to you...it helped. Believe it or not, I feel better. I got to tell my side and hear someone else agree with me that the whole situation was messed up."

"That's probably why people tell you not to bottle things up inside."

I rolled my eyes. "Got it, Dr. Phil," I joked. "But seriously, thank you for listening. I hadn't intended to put all that out there tonight."

"Thank you for confiding in me," he said. "So, you're helping at Benny's but that is temporary. Do you know what you want to do after that."

"Are you wondering if I'm going to stick around?"

"Well, now that you mention it, yeah but I honestly am just trying to get to know you again Tess."

"Fair enough, I get that," I said. No good was going to come from keeping it to myself. "I was offered a job in New York City. A good job."

There was a quick look of shock and maybe something else that flashed across Jack's face. But, he squashed it quickly and was looking at me with no apparent emotion.

"Wow, that was...fast," he said.

"It was. Much faster than expected."

"So, are you taking it? Moving to New York?"

Luckily, the waiter came out with our salads right then, giving me a few minutes of reprieve. After he placed our food in front of us and left, I still didn't respond. I didn't want Jack to misconstrue what I had decided. I was trying to gather my thoughts, but I took too long. And he took he took my silence the wrong way.

"Listen, Tess, I'm not trying to pressure you to stay. When we planned this date, I didn't know you had a job offer in New York."

"Relax Jack, I know you didn't know because no one did at that time. You are the first person I told."

"You haven't told Benny?" he asked.

"No, not yet. I wanted to think about it, figure out what I want for my life, and make up my own mind. And with everything else going on, between Leigh's funeral, Benny's shop, trying to reconnect with everyone I pushed away..." I trailed off.

"There was a lot going on," Jack agreed.

"There was."

"Things are calming down now though," he said.

"I know. And, I've had time to think it over. Prioritize. I turned down the job this morning."

Jack let out a breath that I'm not sure he knew he was holding. He stopped clenching the wrapping of dinnerware in his hand and got down to pulling the silverware out and putting the napkin on his lap.

"And you're sure that's what you want?" he asked.

"I am," I said without any hesitation. "It's actually a relief to not have it hanging over my head anymore."

"Tess..."

"Before you say anything Jack, I didn't say no to the job because of you. Or, at least not because of this," I said gesturing between us with my hand. "I said no because of reconnecting with you as friends, because of having family dinner at your house, getting teased by Max and talking to your mom, because of living with Benny again and actually having a relationship with my brother like I used to before our parents died and I turned into a zombie. Because of having Uncle Rob back and Ruby and being there for Leigh's parents..."

I paused and took a breath and shrugged. "I had a lot of reasons to say no," I finished. "All the reasons I had to say yes, and I know there were some, but they just didn't stack up."

"Well, I'm not going to lie, I'm glad you are staying," Jack said. "Not just for me but for everyone. Benny doesn't say anything, but I know he's so happy to have his little sister back. We've all missed you. Maybe don't be in such a rush to hire someone at Benny's. You can do that until you find another job closer to home."

"Well, I do have a plan. Or, at least an idea." I let that hang for a minute.

"Okay, an idea is good. Care to share?" Jack asked.

I sighed and gave voice to the internal debate I was having.

"I like to cook," I said.

"Hence working in a restaurant," Jack said. "And..." he prompted me to continue.

"In addition to my major in hotel and restaurant management, I took some culinary classes in college and continued taking classes around Arlington when I wasn't working. I've always loved cooking, even when I was younger."

"I remember," Jack said between bites. "So, you are looking at a culinary opportunity?"

I became momentarily distracted watching his strong arms and hands cut up his salad and take a bite. A brief flashback of the kiss we shared in my kitchen the other night flashed through my head, being incased in his arms and the slight brush of his hand on mine. His hands aren't soft and never will be, I don't care what moisturizer he uses. Manual farm labor gave him strong hands and arms and I always thought they were perfect.

It took me a minute to realize he'd asked me a question. He looked at me and gave me a little grin when he caught me staring. I felt my face flush and I quickly focused on my own salad as I thought about my answer.

"There aren't a lot of restaurants around home unless you come to Harrisonburg," I said shrugging.

"So, are you thinking of opening your own restaurant?" he asked.

"Possibly, eventually, but I was thinking something smaller scale to start out. Food trucks are a big thing in D.C. and northern Virginia. It wouldn't require as much money up front, and I could move around to where the lunch and dinner crowds are."

Jack didn't immediately respond. He ate some of his salad and seemed to be deciding if he thought my idea had merit. I pushed my salad around the plate with my fork and tried to be patient waiting on him to respond.

"What kind of food would you serve?" he asked finally.

"For a food truck, I'd want to keep it somewhat simple," I replied. "Sandwiches - specialty sandwiches, gourmet macaroni and cheese, potato and pasta salads, fresh homemade pickles. I'd take a page from Leo and try to source as much as possible locally."

He nodded as I talked, so I felt encouraged that he seemed to like what I was saying.

"So, do you think it's too crazy or risky?" I asked.

"No, not at all," he said. "I think it's a brilliant idea, actually. Not that it matters what I think. You are passionate about it, believe in it, that's what matters."

I nodded and took a bite of salad. I know what he said was true, but it was still good to hear someone else say your idea was viable.

The server brought our dinner and topped off our wine.

"How are things going working for your parents on the farm?" I asked when we were alone again.

I swirled some beef tenderloin in the white wine sauce and put a piece on his plate. He held up his fork with a bite of pork chop and fed it to me. It was cooked perfectly of course. He spent a couple more minutes picking at his food. I wondered if he was going to answer me.

"Things on the farm are good," he said.

I waited for more. After a minute, it was apparent he was not intending to be more forthcoming.

"Good is good I guess." I hesitantly tried to catch his eyes which were stubbornly focused on his plate. He put his fork down and sat back in his chair with a sigh.

"It's like nothing changed," he said.

There were a number of ways to interpret that statement, so I stayed silent until he elaborated.

"Besides a few added responsibilities. I took over because T.J. is getting the horse business going, but I'm doing the same things I did in high school. I literally graduated from high school on a Saturday and went to work on the farm Monday doing the same things I had done the week before, just more of it and for longer hours. I drive the same truck. Do you know it has 300,000 miles? Live in the same bedroom..."

He trailed off, but I could fill in the rest for him. "And you're on a date with the same girl," I said quietly, setting down my fork on my plate. The tenderloin that had seemed so juicy and melt-in-your-mouth tender a minute ago, now sat like lead in my stomach.

"I thought you liked working on the farm. Even when you were fighting battles with your parents to take another photography class or get a new piece of equipment, you insisted it was just a hobby, that you didn't want to do it professionally."

"I know," he said, "but maybe I was trying to convince myself as much as anyone else."

I took a sip of wine and waited for him to open up. This was what I had been sensing from him all night. Something happened, and it was weighing him down.

"Come on Jack, spill it."

"Victoria called me the other day," he said with a sigh.

"Victoria?"

"The grad student from JMU I was dating a year ago."

"A year ago? I didn't know it was that recent."

"It didn't seem important," he said. "I hadn't heard from her. I thought it was long over."

"But it's not over," I said, with a sinking feeling in my stomach.

Jack picked up his napkin and laid it over his plate. He'd only eaten half his food, but I was with him. My appetite was gone too.

"She called. She wants me to come to Colorado. There's a contract position for a photographer at her work. It's a small company, and she convinced them to give me a chance. She showed them my website, and it impressed them, evidently."

I picked up my wineglass and sat back in my chair.

"You want to go?" I asked.

"Yes, and no. It's something different and I guess I've always wondered if I could make it professionally."

"What about Victoria?" I asked. "This isn't just a job opportunity."

"We didn't end badly," he said and sighed. "I've thought about her since she left."

"If I hadn't come home, would there be any question?"

"Probably not," he said without hesitation.

"So, why this?" I asked indicating the table with our half-eaten dinner.

"Because you did come back," he said, banging his hands on the table. The dishes rattled and the wax in the candle sloshed as the flame flickered.

I didn't outwardly react to his outburst but on the inside, I had a sinking feeling in my gut. Jack didn't do outbursts. He was usually the calm one in any situation.

"Tess, I could be perfectly happy working the rest of my life on the farm, dating you, even eventually getting married and building a life together. That's all I ever wanted, and I thought that's how we would go until everything fell apart between you and me in high school."

"But..."

"But things did fall apart, and you moved away, and I did have to consider a different life." He took a big gulp of wine.

We sat silently drinking our wine for a few minutes, each of us lost in our thoughts.

"But then you came back," he said. "And now the life I always wanted is within my reach." He stared at the flickering candle.

"But, what if?"

He raised his head. "What if what?" he asked.

"Jack, you're right. I went away, not in the best way, but I did. I was able to go to college, try a career, figure out what I really liked and wanted to do for a living, and where I wanted to be. You didn't do any of that, but you still can. You're 25 years old, you have plenty of time to explore and figure out what you want before thinking about marriage, and kids, and settling down."

The wine was no longer sitting well in my stomach, so I exchanged it for my water glass and took a big gulp.

"I don't want you sitting on our front porch one day wondering what would've happened if you went after photography and tried to make a go of it," I said. "Or if Victoria was the one who got away," I added on quietly.

The server came over to pick up our plates. Leo was following him.

"Was everything good?" Leo asked expectantly.

Jack and I both smiled and thanked him for such great service. "We're probably ready for the check," he added, and gave the server his credit card. "You're not staying for dessert?" Leo asked. "We have a great raspberry tart with lemon ice cream," he said trying to tempt us.

"No thanks Leo, we are honestly stuffed," I said.

The server came back with Jack's card, and I gave Leo a quick hug while Jack paid.

Leo looked worried but wisely said nothing. He just nodded and squeezed my arms reassuringly, then turned to Jack and shook his hand.

He wished us both a good night as we headed out of the restaurant.

# Chapter 19

# DIFFERENT PATHS

*"She took a step and didn't want to take any more, but she did."*

— Markus Zusak, he Book Thief

The fence posts whipped by as I pumped my legs harder around the field. Sweat ran down my face as the sun came up and the air quickly got warmer. I finally slowed to a stop near the gate, taking a minute to catch my breath, and then going into a slow walk to cool down.

I felt my eyes, almost of their own volition, drift to the road, waiting to see a familiar old pickup truck driving down it. But none came. At least, not the one I wanted to see.

Jack dropped me off at home after dinner last night. The ride was quiet. I guess he said everything he needed to at dinner. I'm not sure I did.

I meant it when I said I didn't want to go into a relationship with him when he was wondering what his life would be like if he chose differently. So, I didn't say I wanted him to stay. That I wanted a relationship with him. To start a life together. Did I even have a right to tell him I wanted him to stay? Would he always wonder 'what if?' if he did stay? Maybe. Probably.

A slight breeze blew through the field, cooling my face and body. The pecking of a woodpecker in a nearby tree, and the crickets chirping in the field were the only sounds. I could feel my heart rate slowing down and a calmness came over me, quieting the emotions that had been battling inside me all night. I climbed to the top of the fence and sat, looking over the field, letting my thoughts wander until they settled on a conclusion.

Jack needed to go.

He was right. His life has stayed constant; he'd never shaken things up. And, if he was okay with that and happy, then I would say great, let's see where you and I together might lead.

But he wasn't okay with it. He questioned why he's never lived in a different room than the one he grew up in, if he's missing out by not going after photography as a career, or even just living someplace new with different people. And with a different lover than the one he's known since he was in the second grade.

He needed to go.

Plus, I had to get things figured out for myself. Maybe it wasn't meant to be for us. Time would tell. Glancing at my watch, I realized I only had an hour to get home, get showered, and get to the shop for work.

Hopping off the fence, I rushed over to my trusty, slightly rusty Corolla and got her started up and seatbelt on as quickly as possible. Me and the Corolla bounced out of the field, onto the gravel drive, and down the road to home.

Freshly showered and dressed in my McCabe's Garage button-down shirt, I waited behind the counter for customers to come in as Benny and Uncle Rob unlocked the front door and opened the garages. Almost as soon as soon as they had opened, Ruby came bustling through the door with an enormous basket of muffins and fruit.

"Hey Ms. Ruby, what is all this?" I asked, running over to help her. I grabbed the basket out of her arms and set it on the counter before the whole thing spilled onto the floor.

"Well, I know Benny got approved for the business loan so he can start taking over and I just wanted to do something for you all to celebrate," she said in one long, nearly out of breath, statement.

"Aw, thank you! This is great!" I said and wasted no time snagging a blueberry muffin for myself.

The sound of a car being pulled into the garage came through the service door behind the counter, and I saw a customer walk by the window toward the front door. Ruby noticed too, so quickly put the basket out with napkins and paper plates.

"I know you guys are busy, so I'll be going. Have a great day," she said while giving me a quick kiss on the cheek before running out the door. I snagged a couple of muffins and some fruit to put under the counter and save for Benny and Uncle Rob before greeting the day's first customer.

Later that evening, Benny and I sat on the front porch sipping a beer and watching the sky turn to night. I was in my comfiest, oldest, thread-bare pajamas that I refused to throw away and Benny was in his favorite flannel pajama bottoms and old AC/DC t-shirt. It was quiet except for the creaking of the old front porch swing we sat on. It was the same porch swing we sat on as kids at my grandmother's house. Grandma was not rich in material goods—most of her stuff was hand-me-downs from relatives or yard sale scores—but what she had we kept and treasured.

"Are you going to keep the same name?" I asked Benny, breaking the peaceful silence.

He sat for a minute and stared at the fireflies that were holding their nightly dance in the yard before responding.

"I think so." He shrugged and took another sip of the beer he'd been nursing since we sat down. Leaning his head back against the swing, he said, "I don't see a point in changing it. It's been McCabe's Garage for nearly 35 years now. People around here know it. I think I'd be shooting myself in the foot if I changed it."

I nodded. "I agree. Plus, it's kind of Uncle Rob's legacy. He put everything he had into that shop."

"Yeah, I know. I just hope he's okay with the other changes that I'd like to make," Benny said.

"He saw the business plan and you've been talking to him about it, I assume, for some time now. Uncle Rob isn't known for being shy or holding back. He'd let you know if he thought you were going in the wrong direction."

"That's true," Benny said with a chuckle. We sat in silence for a little while longer. I finished my beer and was getting ready to go inside when Benny said, "I ran into Jack today."

My forward momentum stopped as if someone had me on a leash and just yanked on it. I collapsed back into the swing somewhat dramatically, and tipped my head back so I was staring at the porch ceiling, mimicking Benny's pose.

"I could've gone all day without hearing the name Jack."

"So, it's like that?" Benny asked, looking at me out of the corner of his eye.

I sighed, loudly. "No... maybe... I don't know. He has things he wants to do. Things he needs to do for himself before he can decide he wants to start a relationship with me or even keep working on the farm."

"I didn't know he wasn't happy," Benny said.

"That's the thing. It's not that he's not happy," I said. "He just doesn't know if maybe he could be happier. Maybe there is another life out there for him besides the one he's grown used to."

"Grass isn't always greener," Benny said quietly, almost like he was talking to himself.

I wondered how often he had told himself that over the years but was afraid to ask him. "No, I know firsthand that the grass isn't always greener. But, sometimes, it is. It's a matter of perspective. I think Jack needs to peek over that fence and try to find out for himself. If he doesn't, he may always wonder about it."

"I guess that's true," Benny said. "But I think no matter what, there will always be something that makes you wonder if you should've chosen differently. Everyone has their 'what ifs' but, if you like your place in life, I think that's enough to make the 'what ifs' nothing more than a passing thought you may have on occasion while waiting in line or sitting at a red stoplight."

"Maybe, but some 'what ifs' are bigger than others."

We sat there for a few more minutes and listened to the local night life come out to play. An owl hooted nearby, and a symphony of insects were playing their favorite songs. It was completely dark now and a cloudless sky allowed the Milky Way to show up in all its beauty. The unfiltered view of the night sky would never get old.

"I'm pretty wiped out," Benny said. "I'm going to bed. Are you going to be, okay?"

He looked at me like he was afraid I wouldn't be there in the morning when he woke up. He'd already had to go through one morning of waking up and finding my bedroom empty, my closet cleaned out, and me gone. I would never put him through that again.

"I'm good Benny," I said, trying to reassure him I wasn't the same messed up teenager that had run out on him all those years ago. "Jack is going to do what he needs to do. I've got my own life to focus on as well. It just isn't our time."

He nodded. "Maybe not right now."

"Maybe not never," I said.

"Maybe not," he agreed quietly.

"Benny, I've been through worse. So have you. We both know life keeps going. This will not break me. I promise."

"I know," he said. He sounded like he meant it. I hoped so. I put Benny through hell in the past. But I survived the loss of my parents, albeit not without scars, but I was still going. I lost Leigh. Jack leaving hurts but I can put that pain in perspective and not let it wreck me.

"Go to bed. I might watch a movie or something since we're off tomorrow."

"Okay, enjoy," he said. "See you in the morning."

When he was inside, I pulled out my phone and opened the messages app. I quickly texted Jack before I could change my mind and then texted Ruby to see if she wanted me to pick her up for church tomorrow.

When I finally went inside the house, I wondered what movie to watch and looked forward to a day off work.

----

"It was good to see the Shays at church," I said to Ruby as she drove us to her house for lunch. If I knew Ruby, that lunch would probably come with a big side of gossip. Ruby ended up picking me up that morning as the trusty, rusty Corolla gave up the effort to be trusty anymore. It wouldn't start. Benny and Uncle Rob towed it to the shop and were working on it right now. I had a bad feeling it would not be good news. Buying a new car did not exactly fit into my plans for all the money I saved during my many years of self-imposed exile and not having a life.

"I'm glad they were there," Ruby said. "I've been checking on them now and then. Trying to make sure they are okay but not make a nuisance of myself. I'm sure some days are worse than others, but they are trying to keep going for Leigh. She would've wanted them to be happy."

"More than anything. I've called and talked to Mrs. Shay a couple of times but haven't been over for a visit since we took her to lunch."

"You've been busy and now you're working at the shop. I've been keeping her updated. She knows," Ruby said.

"I know, but I need to make the time. Maybe I'll see if she wants to meet for lunch one day. Is she back at work? She doesn't work far from Benny's shop, so we could probably meet somewhere."

"She goes back to work tomorrow," Ruby said. "They're both going back. It will be good for them to get out of the house and back into a routine."

"I'll call her later and try to make plans for lunch," I said as Ruby pulled into her driveway.

We went inside the little Cape Cod house and Ruby made her rounds checking on her two cats, Fred and Wilma, and her green parrot, Captain Jack, named after Johnny Depp's character in Pirates of the Caribbean.

I poured us both some sweet ice tea and looked through the refrigerator for lunch stuff. Ruby had made homemade potato salad and had bought some fantastic, salted ham, judging by the piece I stole on the long trip from the refrigerator to the table. Some deli-style brown mustard and baby Swiss cheese on homemade rolls completed the sandwiches, or so I thought, until I saw the crown jewel in her refrigerator.

"I love that woman," I said to myself as I grabbed the jar of her homemade canned pickles that were chilling and just waiting for me to find them.

I smiled as I put the pickles on the table with everything else. It was good to be home. Even though it had not been all sunshine and rainbows, especially with Leigh's death and memorial and now Jack possibly moving away, it didn't change the fact I was happy to be home. I felt like me again. I felt like I was living again. Life—with all its ups and downs—was welcome over the mere existing I had been doing for all those years. As we sat down to eat, I made a mental note to get Ruby's recipe for her potato salad. It might just come in handy one day soon, I hoped.

The sun was getting lower in the sky and evening setting in when Ruby drove me home. We had an excellent lunch and then went to

Grand Caverns and walked along one of the hiking trails that ran through the park. Luckily, I still had a dresser of clothes and shoes at Ruby's house from when I was younger. And they still fit, which was a bonus. Hiking in my flats and dress I wore to church would not have worked well. Now, I was tired and looking forward to a shower and my pajamas. But, as we pulled up outside Benny's house, it became apparent that I would not get either anytime soon.

"Well, at least your car is fixed," Ruby said as we both stared out the window at the person sitting on my front porch in my grandma's old swing, nervously twisting an old baseball hat in his hands. The hat was well worn and didn't look like it could take the abuse for much longer.

To Ruby's point, my car was parked out front in the driveway. Hopefully, that meant Uncle Rob and Benny had fixed it. I don't think Benny would bring it back home if it didn't run. We did not need a rusty Corolla as a lawn ornament.

Ruby pulled to a stop behind my car and waved to Jack. He stood and waved back but didn't make a move to leave the porch. He stared at me and I stared back at him through the windshield.

"I think he wants to talk to you," Ruby said after a minute, when I didn't make a move to get out of the car.

"Right," I said quietly. I leaned over and gave Ruby a hug. "Thank you for lunch. It was excellent. And thanks for the leftovers."

"You're welcome sweetie," she said, hugging me back. "Good luck with whatever this is about."

"I didn't feel like talking about it earlier. I'll fill you in later."

She nodded. "I'm here whenever you need me."

"I know, thank you, love you."

"Love you too." She gave my hand a squeeze before I got out of her car.

I trudged up to the porch as Ruby turned around in the driveway and left. Though I stared at the ground and deliberately did not look at Jack, I could feel his eyes on me as I made my way to the front steps. Finally, I didn't have a choice but to lift my eyes to his.

"Hey Jack," I said with resignation.

"Hey."

He said nothing else for what felt like an eternity. I could see him struggling with how to start.

"Did you have a good time with Ruby?" he asked.

Small talk. I guess that was one way for him to get started.

"Yeah," I said. "Where's Benny?"

"He said he had to run out and do some things, but to tell you he would be home soon."

"He left you sitting on the front porch?"

"No, door's open," he replied. "I just felt like sitting out here. It's a nice evening."

"I'm going to put these leftovers in the fridge and get a glass of wine. Do you want a beer?"

"Sure," he said. "Do you need any help?"

"No, I've got it." As I went through the door, I made sure it closed behind me. A not-so-subtle hint to give me a little space. I needed a few minutes to myself. Shoving the leftovers inside the refrigerator, I closed the door and leaned my head against the cool metal. I didn't want to face what was coming. I had just laid one best friend to rest and now was going to have to say goodbye to another. And it was not lost on me I was the one that left them first.

I took a deep breath and went through the motions of pouring a glass of wine and grabbing a cold beer for Jack. Taking another deep breath, I went back out onto the front porch. Jack still sat on the swing, quietly staring out into the yard. He didn't even look my way as I came back out.

"Hey, you okay?" I asked as I walked over and sat down next to him.

"Huh? Yeah, I'm fine," he said. "Just lost in thought." He took the beer I offered and twisted the cap off. "Thanks."

I sat back against the swing and took a sip of wine. The sky was getting darker, and the night had nearly taken over.

"I'm leaving tomorrow," he said.

"Tomorrow?" I said, shocked. "I didn't think you would leave that soon."

"Neither did I," he said. "But they need someone right away for this position and if I can't get there this week, they are going to find someone else."

"Wow, how did your parents take it?" I asked.

He shrugged. "It took some talking, but they came around. They were a little shocked too, that I'm leaving so soon. But they understand my need to give it a try. They said they would make it work on the farm without me. Reminded me I can always come home whenever I wanted."

"You know that," I said. "Just like I knew I could come home to Benny."

He nodded. "Yeah, I know."

"I want you to know that I'm not leaving to be with Victoria," he said. "I don't know how I feel about her anymore. This is more about this opportunity and not passing it up."

"You need to go. I don't want you to stay here and always wonder what if. First and foremost, we're friends, Jack. We have been since the second grade, we grew up together, you were my first lover, and have been my only true love. I will not be the one to hold you back."

He leaned his head back and drained the rest of his beer and set it down on the porch. He looked over at me. The light from the porch light bathed us both in a yellow glow.

"I'll miss you," he said. "I'll let you know how I'm doing. What I'm doing."

"Okay." I met his gaze. He leaned towards me, and I met him halfway. When we met in the middle, the kiss wasn't one of passion or two lovers reuniting. It was tender. It was goodbye.

We pulled back, and he stood up. He headed down the porch steps and stopped. Turning back, he said, "We went our separate ways once before, but we came back together. We could do it again. Paths are funny like that. We could be on different paths now, but who knows down the road. They could come together again."

"Yes, but will we be at an intersection or will we be running parallel again like we used to? That's the question," I said.

He nodded and looked down at the ground. "I guess that's true," he said. "Only time will tell. Later Tessie."

"Later Jack."

I sat on the porch and finished my wine as he turned his truck around and went down the driveway towards the road.

# Chapter 20

# GHOSTS OF THE PAST

*"I don't care about whose DNA has recombined with whose. When everything goes to hell, the people who stand by you without flinching--they are your family."*
— Jim Butcher, Proven Guilty

"**M**y breaks are shrieking at me every time I stop at a light..."

"I need an oil change..."

"I need an inspection and need to be at work at 9. Can Benny get me in...?"

The morning at Benny's shop had been crazy. I barely had time to think about Jack leaving today.

Barely.

It was always there, a lingering thought in the back of my head despite all of my brave words about not holding him back and having to find my own path and blah blah blah...

The fact was, if I thought about him leaving too much, I would probably fall apart. This would not be good for Benny's business to have his sister a blubbering mess in the middle of a busy morning. Word must have got around that Benny officially took over the shop from Uncle Rob and people wanted to be supportive. Apparently, being supportive means if their car was making any kind of "funny little clanging sound" in the past six months, they were bringing it in this morning.

I was happy for Benny, truly, but the morning had been a lot and I needed a break. I was hiding in the back of the garage where we had a little room with a refrigerator, microwave, and small table that had seen better days. It could really use some sprucing up. The microwave looked like it might be one of the first ones ever invented, and the refrigerator door had more scuff marks on it than the garage floor. Both Benny and my Uncle Rob had the habit of grabbing what they needed out of it and then kicking the door shut with their black work boots.

I was busy making plans to clean up and redecorate a bit when Uncle Rob came in to join me for lunch. John, one of Uncle Rob's best friends and former employee of the shop for more years than I can count, was watching the front for me. He retired a few years back, but still came in nearly every day to see Uncle Rob and Benny and chat with the customers. The shop was his home. He was comfortable here. And his wife might kill him if he hung out at home all day bugging her.

"Hey Tess," Uncle Rob said as he came in the room. He grabbed a bag lunch out of the refrigerator and kicked the door shut. I rolled my eyes.

"What?" he asked.

"That door is going to fall off one day from you and Benny kicking it shut. And its nearly black from all the scuff marks."

"That just gives it character," he said with a smile.

"No, that is not character. I will give this room character when I fix it up," I replied.

"Tess, I've got way too much else to be doing and spending money on to worry about fixing up the break room right now," Benny said as he entered the room to grab his own lunch. And like clockwork, he kicked the poor refrigerator door closed.

I just shook my head.

"I'm not asking you to pay for it. I have money saved up and it won't take much," I said cutting Benny off when he tried to say something. "I'm not redoing floors and counters or anything, just going to clean it up and maybe get a microwave from this century at Walmart. That thing is a health hazard."

Both my uncle and my brother looked at the microwave and shrugged.

"Heats my leftover meatloaf surprise just fine," Uncle Rob said.

"Yes, it only takes 15 minutes," I deadpanned.

My uncle and I could banter back and forth like this all day, so Benny broke in to bring us around to talking about more important shop business than the decor of the break room.

"I'm going over to the salvage yard after closing," he said. "I've finished with the inventory. There are a lot of parts that we can use for repairs here and list on-line for sale. Tess, I was wondering if you can help me. Do you know anything about redoing a website? We have a basic one now, but I'd like to revamp it."

"I know a bit. I did some website work for the newspaper in college but I'm not a professional by any stretch of the imagination," I said. "Let me search for a professional. You need a better website than I can create Benny."

I could see my brother adding up the cost of paying someone to redo the website in his head. In the grand scheme of things, the ancient appliances in the break room were probably not a priority.

"I will search and get quotes and meet with people," I said. He had a lot on his plate. Hopefully, this would help with some of his stress. I wondered if him getting that loan was a blessing or a curse. My brother went from calm and easygoing to looking like he had the weight of the world on his shoulders overnight. But it wasn't the first time that happened to him. If he could survive losing his parents and becoming responsible for raising an emotional headcase of a teenager all in one night, he could do this.

A memory flashed in my head of a day not long after my parents died. It had been about a week since we officially gave the keys to my parents' house to the bank and walked away. The house and land were for sale and the bank was auctioning off the equipment and cattle. We were still unpacking in the house that -- through years of fixing up and care -- Benny managed to turn into the home we live in now. Boxes were everywhere. It was late at night, and I was still awake. Even though it was our fifth night in the house, I still hadn't got used to the unfamiliar room and being the only one upstairs by myself. I quietly made my way down the stairs with my pillow to sleep on the couch instead. I thought Benny was in bed already, but when I came around the corner to go into the living room, he was there. He was leaning forward, his elbows resting on his knees and his head in his hands looking at the floor. For a second, I thought about going over and sitting next to him, to comfort him, but I didn't think he would want that. My brother didn't share his emotions easily, not even with me. After a minute, I quietly made my way back upstairs.

Now, back in the breakroom, watching him eat his lunch, I could see some of the same tension in him I saw that night. Not the grief, thankfully, but the stress.

After our much-needed break, we all went back to our respective tasks. The pace picked up at the front desk again in the afternoon as people were getting off work, but it made the hours fly by. I really didn't have time to think about Jack too much until the day was over. I locked the front door and gratefully flipped the sign to closed. Leaning against the door with exhaustion and staring out at the darkening sky, it hit me, Jack would be long gone by now.

I knew that dwelling on it could suck me down into a dark hole. Between Leigh's death and Jack moving away, I had lost my two best friends in the world in a span of a couple weeks. But I would not go back into that place I was for so many years after my parents died.

Turning back toward the garage, toward my brother and my uncle, toward the life full of possibilities that was open to me, I thought about helping Benny build his dream and my own dreams that I worked on during quiet times. I thought about Ruby, Uncle Rob, Leigh's parents. I had a life here, and I was determined to live it. With these thoughts, I felt my heart get a little lighter.

Making my way to the garage, I heard Uncle Rob and Benny talking and laughing about something. Ready to go join them, a knock on the front door of the shop halted my forward progress mid-stride. I had just locked and displayed the sign telling everyone we were closed on that very same front door. Groaning and taking a deep breath, I turned around ready to tell a customer to please come back tomorrow, when I saw who it was at the door and stopped dead in my tracks.

Lexie Blake.

She couldn't seriously be here.

I liked to think of myself as mostly a nice person. A kind person. I don't kick puppies or throw rocks at kids, I'm not an Internet troll, I don't run over pedestrians. I would take dealing with someone who does all of those things over Lexie Blake. If there was a person on this planet that made my blood boil the second I saw her, it was Lexie Blake.

I stared at her for a moment standing outside the door in the waning evening light and seriously considered if anyone would miss her if I ran her over with my newly tuned up Toyota. To say I disliked this woman was an understatement. I reigned in my homicidal thoughts and slowly came around the corner of the front desk, went back to the front door, and unlocked it. I left her to do the opening part herself.

"Tess," she said quietly but evenly.

"Lexie," I said just as quietly and evenly.

I gave her a moment. When she said nothing, I decided to move this along.

"What do you want?" I asked none too friendly.

"Is Benny here?" She had the audacity to ask the question, as if one, she didn't know that he was in fact here and two, she had any business asking anything about my brother.

"Not for you he's not," I replied.

"Tess," she started, but I put my hand up, cutting her off.

"Guess what? I don't care. Whatever it is. I don't want to hear it and I don't care. Your car could be burning to bits on the side of the road, and I wouldn't call the fire department. So whatever it is, I suggest you take it somewhere else and stay the hell away from my brother."

My voice rose steadily as I ripped into her so that by the time I got to the end of my tirade (or hissy fit depending on your perspective), I was essentially shouting at her.

Of course, my brother and uncle heard this and decided to come out to see what was going on.

"Tess, Tess, stop," my brother ran over and stood between me and Lexie with his hands up to keep us apart. Then, he turned to Lexie and apologized to her for my behavior!

My mind went blank. I think I was in shock because I could not believe what I was seeing. I looked at Uncle Rob. He glanced away and wouldn't meet my eyes.

"What the hell Benny!?" I screeched, finally finding my voice again.

"Tess, you've been gone a long time, things change, people change," he said, turning around to look at me.

"The past doesn't change Benny," I retorted. "She dropped you like a bad habit as soon as things got hard, when you needed her the most, that didn't change."

"We've talked Tess, we've been talking for a while," he replied. "There was a lot going on then that you don't know about. We talked through things and we still care about each other."

I was silent. My eyes couldn't believe what they were seeing, and my ears couldn't believe what they were hearing. My brother had lost his parents, become guardian of his little sister, and needed to find a place to live after the bank foreclosed on the farm, and that's when his girlfriend of nearly three years decided she couldn't handle it all and dumped him. Up to the point things went to crap, they had been talking about a life together, getting married, where they would live. And she dumped him and left town when he needed her the most.

When I needed her the most.

I had loved Lexie. I couldn't wait to get dressed up and stand at the altar and watch her marry my brother.

And she left us both at the lowest time of our life.

When I finally found my voice, I could barely look my brother in the eyes.

"You may have talked things through and forgiven her," I said to him quietly before turning my gaze on Lexie.

"I have not."

I turned around and grabbed my stuff from under the counter and left through the garage. No one said anything to me or tried to stop me.

# Chapter 21

# New Beginnings

*"Listen to the mustn'ts, child. Listen to the don'ts.*
*Listen to the shouldn'ts, the impossibles, the won'ts.*
*Listen to the never haves, then listen close to me...*
*Anything can happen, child. Anything can be."*

— Shel Silverstein

S C R O M L E T. I typed the letters in a decorative font on my laptop. Maybe I was getting ahead of myself by planning a menu for my food truck and/or cafe that I wanted to open, but it was all I felt like thinking about right now. Work today had been unpleasant and awkward.

I didn't see Benny after my outburst the night before and I avoided him and Uncle Rob as much as a person could avoid people they worked with and needed to interact with professionally all day. I gave them tickets, relayed customer concerns, got feedback, relayed that to the customers, and that was it.

It sucked.

All because of Lexie James.

Scromlet - *A cross between an omelet and scrambled eggs, a scromlet is what many people end up with when they try to make an omelet. At Tess' Cafe (work on the name later), we decided to skip the stress and embrace the beauty of the scromlet. Three eggs scrambled to fluffy perfection and topped with the ingredients of your choosing and then smothered in your favorite cheese.*

I italicized the description and eyeballed my handiwork. All in all, I was pretty happy with it. Tess' Cafe was a nice name for an actual brick and mortar building but less so for a food truck. As I still wasn't sure which way I was going to swing - and that largely depended on funding - I needed a name that would work for both.

Laying my head back on the porch swing, I sighed and looked up at the stars that were really starting to show in all their glory in the darkening night sky.

It was getting late. Benny still wasn't home.

I was about to break down and try to call him when I heard the familiar sounds of gravel crunching under tires. A couple of seconds later, I saw headlights shining way down the driveway from a very familiar-looking Jeep. Benny was home.

I watched as he slowly made his way up the driveway and parked next to my car. When he got out, he had a paper bag in his hand. I set my laptop aside as he came up on the porch and sat down next to me.

He handed me the bag. Opening it, I saw my favorite ice cream, Rocky Road, inside.

"Peace offering," he mumbled.

"Thanks," I said. "I'm sorry, too. To you and Uncle Rob. I hate being in arguments with you both, and it's not either of you I'm mad at."

"I know. So does Uncle Rob."

We sat there quietly for a minute. I had a thousand questions going through my mind and an inner debate on whether I could ask them. My good side was making the argument that this wasn't something I could pry into. If Benny wanted to share with me what was going on between him and Lexie, he would've talked to me about it already. My bad side wanted to tell my good side to shut its pie hole, because I wanted some answers on why the hell he was letting her back into his life.

After a few minutes of absolute silence, Benny opened the door. Admittedly, he only cracked it open, but that was all I needed.

"There was a lot you missed while you were away, Tess," Benny said.

"I understand that, but I was there when she abandoned you, abandoned us, when we needed her the most," I replied. The anger was building up again. I could feel it rising from my gut and making its way to my chest.

Breathe. Tess, just breathe. I repeated this to myself in my head as I took many deep breaths. Benny must have thought I lost my mind.

After taking a few breaths and counting to 256 in my head, I beat the anger down so I didn't blow up again. Truthfully, my anger surprised me. I wasn't a person who normally showed my anger in explosive, door slamming, glass breaking types of ways. I was the silent, angry type that bottled everything up for a therapist to work out an indeterminate amount of time later in my life. Though, perhaps my running away from home and alienating everyone I knew and loved for years had proved that not to be the healthiest method for handling emotions.

After gaining some semblance of control, I felt like I could contribute to the conversation in a productive manner again.

"When did she come home?" I asked calmly, though my voice sounded a little strained and odd, even to my own ears.

"She got back about six months ago," Benny replied. "Her house has been shut up this whole time. They had a cousin or something from up in Staunton come check on the place every couple of months, but that's it. No one had been there to stay until Lexie came back."

I nodded, and the anger inside quieted down. Wow, I guess I was so wrapped up in my pain back then that I didn't know Lexie's whole family had packed up and left.

"You didn't realize it wasn't just Lexie that left, did you?" Benny asked.

When did he become a mind reader?

"Her whole family packed up and left overnight," Benny continued. "No notice to jobs, no goodbyes to friends, not even a forwarding address. They were just gone."

"Wow, I guess I didn't know that. How did I not know that?"

"Your entire world had just been flipped on its head Tess, I don't think you were aware of much else going on around you," Benny replied.

"Did she explain what happened? Where she went? Why she came back?" I asked, now more curious and, frankly, concerned than angry. "They must have been in some sort of trouble to up and leave like that."

"That's what everyone thinks, and they aren't wrong," Benny said. "She hasn't told me much, just that her dad had got caught up in something and got in over his head. He feared for his family's safety, so they picked up and left."

"Is there no more fear of danger?" I asked quietly.

"I don't think so. Her mother passed three years ago, sick with cancer, and her father passed last winter from a heart attack. Whatever sins he had, he's paid for them."

"Lexie was their only child, so she inherited everything. She came back to check out the house and see what she was dealing with, and she hasn't left," Benny finished with a shrug.

I let everything Benny said sink in and realized I was probably the one in the wrong here.

"I'll apologize to her," I said.

"I don't think she expects an apology, but I would appreciate it," Benny said.

We sat there quietly, pushing my grandmother's swing back and forth with our feet and staring at the stars.

"I'm tired," I said, as a wave of exhaustion washed over me.

Benny nodded. "Me too."

"I have something to run by you tomorrow, you and Uncle Rob," I said.

"Does it have anything to do with Tess' Cafe?" Benny asked and nodded at the laptop still sitting open next to me. I had forgotten it was there.

"That's a working title," I said. "But, yes. It's an idea I'm kicking around."

"Good," Benny said. "Kick those ideas around long enough and you end up doing something with them. Put some work into it, and you might have a good thing started."

I smiled at him. "You would know."

"Come on, kid, let's get some shuteye," Benny said. "Tomorrow's another busy day."

# Chapter 22

# LETTING GO

*"You attend the funeral, you bid the dead farewell. You grieve. Then you continue with your life. And at times the fact of her absence will hit you like a blow to the chest, and you will weep. But this will happen less and less as time goes on. She is dead. You are alive. So live."*

— Neil Gaiman, Fables & Reflections

I stared down at my parents' gravestones. This was the first time I'd visited since I came home. There was a bouquet of sunflowers on my mother's grave. Benny had been here recently. I wondered how often he came.

"I'm sorry," I whispered. Even though I was alone in the cemetery, it seemed like I should talk quietly, similar to how you would in the sanctuary at church. It was sacred ground.

"After you died, I lost who I was and didn't behave the way you taught me."

I could feel the lump in my throat already. Tears rolled down my cheeks. I hadn't been here for five minutes. So much for keeping it together. I don't know why I ever thought I could.

I sat down between their graves.

"Hopefully, Leigh is with you. She was taken from us too soon, but I feel better knowing she's up in Heaven with you. I hope that comforts her parents some too. It was her death that finally brought me back home. She never gave up on me, never gave up trying to get me back. In the end, she finally succeeded."

I sat there quietly for some time, lost in my memories of Leigh. My mind kept jumping around from remembering camping trips to going to the mall to just hanging out watching movies. The grief could overwhelm me if I let it, but I refused. I hated Leigh was gone. I hated it took her death for me to finally come home. But I was not going down that dark hole again where I lost myself and forgot to live. To pull myself back from the abyss of grief that I knew all too well could swallow me whole, I changed the subject.

"I guess Benny has probably already told you he bought Uncle Rob's shop and he bought a salvage yard, too. He's got some big plans. I didn't realize how ambitious he was until I helped him with the business plan. He's been thinking about this for a long time, just waiting for the right opportunity. I was so stuck in my own crap, I never thought about what Benny wanted. I figured he was happy working for Uncle Rob and living in the house he got for us after you died."

I plucked some blades of grass and twisted it between my fingers. They were smooth and cool to the touch despite the warm spring day. Every day was getting warmer, and it wouldn't be long before we were amid another hot Virginia summer.

"Jack is gone too," I whispered. "I've been trying to hold up and not let people see how much I miss him. He left about a month ago. At first, he was texting and calling a lot. Sending pictures of what he was seeing and telling me about Colorado. But, after a few days, it became less. Then, it was more brief texts than calls. Now, I haven't heard from him in two weeks."

"I had to let him go. I could've asked him to stay, but we both would've been wondering if that was what he wanted. He needed to take this shot. I know that. I know it was the right thing. Just like it was the right thing for me when I left, even if the manner in which I left wasn't the best."

I pulled my knees up and laid my head on them while my hands incessantly pulled up blades of grass. There was going to be a bare patch in the grass soon if I didn't stop.

"I just miss him."

Picking my head up off my knees, I took a deep breath and looked at the clear blue sky and the mountains that rose to meet it. That was the one thing I always missed when I was living in northern Virginia. The mountains. In the Valley, there are mountains always in the background. Growing up, I took it for granted. They were always there, like sentinels guarding the Valley from invaders. It took me a little while to place why I felt like something was missing whenever I walked around Arlington until one day, it just hit me. There were no mountains to add the perfect backdrop to every photo. Without the mountains, it just never felt like home.

Despite what brought me here, and even though Jack moved away, I was still glad to be home. Even though I still missed my parents so much, it physically hurt in my heart and sometimes I was back where I started, surrounded by constant reminders of them. I was happy. I was finally in a better place and living life again.

"Don't worry about me," I said to my parents. "I'm going to be okay. I have plans of my own. Let me tell you about Tess' Cafe."

I laid back in the grass and stared at the clear blue sky while I told my parents all of my plans for my new business that I was launching. As I talked about my plans, my sadness over Jack leaving melted away and, while still grieving for Leigh, I could put it in the background as my ideas for my future took shape and my excitement over getting started grew.

# Chapter 23

# FOCUS (JACK)

*"An invisible red thread connects those who are destined to meet, regardless of time, place, or circumstance. The thread may stretch or tangle, but will never break."*

— Chinese Proverb

The slight breeze ruffled my hair, and the bright sun warmed my back. I held my breath as the hawk flew into view. The slapping sound of the camera shutter broke the silence as I captured the hawk in a series of images. I was about a mile from Longs Peak in Rocky Mountain National Park in Colorado. I had sold photos here and there in the past, but this was my first professional job as a photographer. That my ex-girlfriend recommended me for the job to get me out here with her more than for my skills as a photographer grated a bit, but I was loving the work so I dealt with it.

I was working with a team of researchers that were studying wildlife in the national parks for a private conservation firm. I had a yearlong contract to provide photography services. It was the opportunity of a lifetime.

And Victoria knew that when she called me.

As soon as I got to Colorado, she wanted to pick up where we had left off. I couldn't blame her. She didn't know things had changed for me. At first, I even tried to deny to myself that my feelings had changed. I asked her to give me some time to settle into my new situation and the studio apartment the company rented for me. Denver, Colorado was our central place of operations, but we were traveling to national, state, and even some local parks all over the country. I didn't think I'd be seeing the apartment a lot.

At first, the nomadic lifestyle was really appealing. For a guy like me who had lived in the same house for his entire life, living out of a suitcase and being constantly on the go was new and exciting. Four months later, part of me still found it to be new and exciting, but another part of me was missing home. It felt like that other part of me that missed the farm, my family, my friends, and especially Tess, seemed to get bigger every day.

I think it was hard on Victoria, too, having to work with me. Thankfully, we were in different departments, so we weren't together day in and day out. I would've had to bow out. That wouldn't have been fair to her. I tried to see if there was still anything between us. At least for me, there just wasn't.

I took her to dinner a few times. We went hiking. We were as compatible as ever, but the feelings I used to have for her were gone. Truthfully, I don't know if they were ever there to begin with. She was an amazing person, beautiful and easy to talk to, and she deserved someone who loved her fully and completely. Not someone who saw her as a good friend who was easy to hang out with.

When Tess came back into my life, I remembered what it was like to truly be crazy about someone, even when it was against your better judgment and that person you were crazy for could drive you crazy. My mom always told me, sometimes life don't make a lick a sense.

I had to get away from home for many reasons. I had to see if I could make it as a photographer. I had to live under a roof that wasn't bought and paid for by my parents. I had to see if those feelings I got the instant I saw Tess sitting in her car in front of my house were real. She had hurt me badly, but it was a long time ago and she was going through a pain that I can't even imagine to this day. It's been six years since then. We've both grown up. And, even though she's thousands of miles away and I haven't seen her in months, my feelings are still there.

I'm going to finish this job. I signed a contract, and I will fulfill it. I'm going to make things right with Victoria, because she is a good friend who I care about. And then, I'm going to go home and I'm going to build a life with the woman I've been in love with since the second grade. If she will have me. It was something to hope for.

# Chapter 24

# CROSSROADS DINER

*"The thing about roads is sometimes you happen upon them again. Sometimes you get another chance to travel down the same path."*
— Jill Santopolo, The Light We Lost

Two levels at the end of a dead-end street. Not a cute little cul-de-sac prevalent all over the suburbs today, just a dead end. It had a porch made of wood planks painted green and a matching green bench swing hanging from the ceiling. Two bedrooms, one bathroom—actually more of an indoor outhouse than a real bathroom. The kitchen had the only running water in the house.

Glamorous, it wasn't. These days, it would probably be condemned. Maybe even then, if anyone with that kind of power had checked it out. No matter. My grandmother's house was my favorite place in the world. It could've been a cardboard box. If Grandma was there, that was where I wanted to be.

Grandma always made me feel like I was the only one in her world. I knew that wasn't true, but it never felt that way. She displayed all the things I made at Sunday school all over her house with pride and if I did some small chore for her, she would act like it was the best thing anyone had ever done.

We did everything together. We walked to the campus of James Madison University because I liked to see the smokestacks and the ducks. We walked to the Farm Bureau and Grandma would buy me stickers. I always tried to find stickers or a key chain that had my name on it. They never did. We walked to Midway, a little mom and pop grocery store behind her house. We walked everywhere. Grandma didn't drive. Grandpa's car sat in front of her house for years after he died. I'm not sure what ever happened to it.

That was a long time ago. Today, I'm standing in a big parking lot around where I think my grandmother's house once stood. That same University Grandma and I would walk to when I was little, bought her house and paved it over to make a parking lot.

Her house is gone. And, the Midway. And, the dead-end street. And, the Farm Bureau.

And Grandma.

I sat down on the place I think my grandmother's house once occupied and leaned against one of my car's tires. The hard metal of the hubcap pressed into the back of my gray hoodie and the cold pavement seeped through my favorite pair of jeans. Under my hoodie was a button down shirt that had Crossroads Diner scrawled across the top left pocket and a bright pink and black logo on the back.

Over the course of the past eight months of building my dream, Tess's Cafe became the Crossroads Diner. Today was the grand opening.

Months of planning and work had led up to this point. I was excited and terrified, exhausted yet unable to rest. Happier than I've been in a long time, yet there was a hint of underlying sadness. Unable to do more than catch a few restless hours of sleep last night, I got up long before dawn and got ready. I left a note for Benny that I was getting an early start, then got in my Toyota – that still runs thanks to my uncle and brother – and left.

I'm not sure what led me to this place. It was a big day for me. But, the closer I got to opening, the more and more I thought about who wouldn't be there to see it. It didn't send me spiraling down a black hole but the feeling that they were missing was always at the back of my mind. It would creep up at odd times. I would think about how Leigh would love that the logo had a big hot pink X in it, and the splashes of pink that were strategically placed around the diner. My mom would have had a great time building the menu with Ruby and me and decorating with her clay pots and vases. Every time Benny or Uncle Rob did something to fix up the diner, I could picture my dad working right next to them. Grandma would've just been enjoying watching it all come together.

"I miss all of you. I wish you could be here. Please wish me luck."

Sighing, I pushed myself off the ground. It was time to get started.

\*\*\*

"Order for table 3 in the window."

Lexie picked up the order and smiled. "Things are going great," she said.

I smiled back. Things were going great. The grand opening had gone well but I knew people would come in for that out of shear curiosity. The test was if they kept coming in after the initial newness had worn off. We've been open for 63 days now (not that I was counting) and we had takeout orders from people picking up a breakfast burrito or sandwich on the way to work and the tables had stayed occupied throughout the morning. As the morning ended, there would be a brief lull but it wouldn't last long. We would be filling up again for lunch by 11:30.

When we opened, Lexie offered to be a server until we could get a staff hired. Now, two and half months later, Lexie hired two more servers and is managing the front end of the house.

"I'm going to start prepping for lunch," I said to Hugo. He gave me a thumbs up as he stood over the flat top finishing the last order we had from the breakfast rush.

The big man was an amazing find and I would forever be grateful to Luis for recommending him. Hugo and Luis were childhood friends but as they got older they went their separate ways in life. Luis of course became the head chef at The Olive Tree but Hugo didn't do so well. He ran into some trouble and did some time in prison. I don't know the details but I know he was able to work in the kitchen while he was there. It was a rough way to learn to cook but he made the most of it. When he got out, he looked Luis up and asked for help finding work. Vito took him on at The Olive Tree and Hugo did amazing by all accounts. So, when I wanted to bring someone on to run the kitchen at the Crossroads Diner, Luis and Hugo drove down. We chatted for hours. Hugo was a natural fit.

Without Lexie and Hugo, I know the Crossroads Diner would not be as successful as its been. If I was the heart of the place, they were its soul. In a way, all three of us were alike in our need for a fresh start. The diner gave us a focus for our life; it was something we could watch grow everyday. I had no doubt they loved the place as much as I did.

All of my friends at The Olive Tree had been hugely supportive. On the long list of people I had to thank for making this dream come true, they were at the top. Vito and his family had driven down from Northern Virginia a few times to see how progress was going, and he was never too tired or busy to answer my calls or texts when I had a question or problem.

Happily separating the hamburger meat I ordered from the Hallowell's farm into portions for hamburger patties and meatloaves and thinking about all the people I had to thank for making this happen, I didn't hear the footsteps behind me. But I did hear Hugo's bellowing voice.

"Hey, can I help you my man? Seating is out there." he said.

I turned around to see what poor person had breached the sanctity of Hugo's kitchen.

Jack.

I dropped the hamburger patty I was forming and it landed in a lump of meat on the floor. Even through my shock, I was calculating what that meat cost that we would now have to throw away.

Hugo stepped in and scooped up the meat off the floor. "You okay boss?" he asked looking me in the eye.

It took me a minute. "Good Lord Tess, pull yourself together," my brain was screaming at me inside my head.

"Yes!" I said a little too loudly. "I'm fine. Hugo this is my friend Jack," I said introducing them. "He's been away doing a photography job. I didn't know he was back in town."

"Okay, now stop talking," my brain said to me. I stopped rambling while Hugo and Jack shook hands.

"I will leave you to it then," Hugo said looking at me like I was a little crazy. "Don't worry about the meat, I'll make my lunch out of it so it doesn't go to waste."

"Hugo, you don't need to use meat off the floor for your lunch," I said.

"It's stupid to let it go to waste," he replied with more than a little attitude. "One, I cleaned that floor myself. It's not that bad. Two, the heat from the grill will further get rid of any dirt. And, three, you know where I came from, I've had worse."

With a nod to me and Jack, he walked off still mumbling to himself about not wasting perfectly good meat.

"Sorry to bother you at work," Jack said. "I just wanted to see the place. When I came in, Lexie told me you were in the kitchen and to go on back. Knowing you were only a few feet away, I couldn't wait any longer to see you."

Still trying to recover from the shock that he was standing in front of me after so long, it took a minute for his words to register in my brain. Then another minute to figure out what to say. Not knowing how to take what he just said, small talk seemed the way to go.

"When did you get back?"

"Last night. Mom and Dad picked me up from Dulles airport."

"They showed me some of your pictures that you sent them. They were really good," I said.

"Thanks," he said. His face lit up. I could see the pride he had in his work. He should be proud. His pictures were phenomenal.

"They kept me up to date on all of this," he said gesturing with his hand around the kitchen.

"Your Mom and Dad were both so amazing. They helped me a lot with finding local food suppliers and getting agreements in place. And your brothers have definitely helped keep the lights on with how much business they've brought in, not only eating here themselves, but also telling anyone who will listen to come here."

"I'm glad they all came through for you. This is really amazing."

The warm feeling I always got when I looked around at the diner and how well it was doing washed over me. Pride in my accomplishment, gratitude and love for everyone helping me, joy at watching something I started grow into a viable business, all of these things made up that warm feeling I got in the pit of my stomach. Realizing that I was standing their smiling like an idiot and not saying anything for way too long, I fumbled for something else to say. I had a million questions going in my head but didn't want to hammer him with all of them.

"Maybe I should go, I know you are busy," he finally said, ending the awkward silence and starting to turn back toward the swinging door that separated the kitchen from the dining area.

"Don't go" I screamed inside my head. Seeing him again brought back all the old feelings that I had been able to push aside and ignore for the past year.

But, maybe his feelings had changed.

"Are you going to be in town for awhile?" I asked, trying to sound nonchalant.

He stopped mid-turn and looked back at me. "I'm back Tess." He hesitated a second and looked at the floor as if he was debating internally if he should say more.

"I missed you."

And, with that simple but loaded statement, he left the kitchen.

My hands were still covered in raw hamburger meat. I was wearing an apron that showed probably every breakfast food I cooked along side Hugo that morning. My hair was falling out of the bun I put it in at 3am when I got up to get to the diner (Yes, 3am! I'm up before Benny now!). As with all the other crucial moments in my life – good and bad – this one was unscripted and unplanned. And, somehow I knew, this moment, right now, would be another – not the last – but definitely another defining moment for me.

Jack was back. He missed me and I had definitely missed him. We both had done things over the past year to grow and find purpose in our life. Build a career, figure out what path we want to take. We were both in a better place than a year ago.

Smiling, I turned back to the hamburger meat and began making patties again.

# Chapter 25

# THE LEAP

*"So it's not gonna be easy. It's going to be really hard; we're gonna have to work at this everyday, but I want to do that because I want you. I want all of you, forever, everyday. You and me... everyday."*
— Nicholas Sparks, The Notebook

I was sitting at one of the tables doing some paperwork while Lexie and Hugo finished closing the diner. It was only 7:30 at night but my day starts at 3a.m., so it was feeling pretty late. In the back of my head, I knew if we started serving dinner, I would be sitting here at 12:30 at night doing this.

Still, the restaurant was doing amazing. The fact that people were wanting us to be open for dinner too was a good problem to have. We just had our best week yet. Some restaurants never get out of the red, there is so much overhead, but we had been open for not even a year yet and were making money.

I officially made Lexie the front end manager. She had more than earned it. In fact, she seemed to be thriving and really enjoy the work. Hugo treated the kitchen like it was his own sacred temple. Only the worthy could enter there. The two kitchen staff we finally were able to hire probably would've had an easier time getting to work in the kitchen at the White House. Hugo was very particular and would settle for nothing less than what he considered the ideal kitchen staff.

Sometimes I felt lucky that I could get in the kitchen. It was like an exclusive club or something. Our kitchen staff completely taking Hugo's lead and ensuring the sanctity of the kitchen. I didn't complain. I couldn't have asked for a more devoted head chef and kitchen manager than Hugo and he picked some amazing people to hire. The kitchen was treated with the utmost respect and care.

I leaned back against the booth seat and stared at the ceiling. With the diner only serving breakfast and lunch, we were well staffed and had a good schedule we could all live with. If we start serving dinner, we will need to bring on at least one or two more managers and multiple more staff. It would be a big undertaking. Still, we were all excited at the idea of a dinner service. Hugo had started making notes for a dinner menu and trying out some recipes. He served them as specials at lunch and all of them so far had been well received and repeatedly requested again.

French onion soup with a French dip sandwich. I jotted the thought down in my notebook. I always made a good French onion soup. I could show Hugo for lunch tomorrow and add it as a possible item for the dinner menu.

All the sudden there was a loud crash in the kitchen and I nearly jumped out of my skin. I was about to get up and rush back there when I heard Lexie laughing.

"You guys okay?" I called.

"Yes," Lexie yelled back, still laughing.

"This woman is a menace. She is no longer allowed in the kitchen," Hugo said as he came through the swinging door that separated the kitchen from the dining area. Lexie was right behind him and more than amused she got under the big man's skin.

"Good luck with that Hugo," I said, grinning at him.

Hugo and Lexie had hit it off from the day one. They had almost a brother/sister type of relationship. Their playful bickering and jabs at each other was fun to watch and always made everyone laugh. Even when we were slammed during the breakfast and lunch rush, the diner had a fun, light-hearted atmosphere that I think attracted people as much as the food.

I think Hugo and Lexie hit it off so well because they had more in common than people may think. Lexie's return to Crossroads had not been well received by a lot of the small town. Rumors swirled about her family and what happened all those years ago. Attitudes have started to thaw with her working at the diner but she wasn't going to be winning any popularity contests soon. Hugo was new here and it took him a while to warm up to people. But, once he did, you had a friend for life.

Headlights flashed across the diner as someone pulled into the parking lot.

"Who can that be? Is Benny coming to get you?" I asked Lexie.

"No, not tonight," she said. She looked a little sad. I wanted to ask her if something was wrong but now was probably not a good time.

"Stay here," Hugo said as he went to the front door to see who was here after closing.

Crossroads was a small town. Most of the crime here was petty and small. But Hugo was a cautious man. He always walked out with Lexie and me and made sure we were in our cars and pulling out of the parking lot before he left.

He looked out the window on the door as whoever had pulled in turned off the headlights. Then I could see the truck and the guy sitting in it through the window next to the booth I was in. Hugo saw him too and raised his eyebrows at me in question.

"What? Who is it?" Lexie asked, running up to peer out the window next to Hugo.

"Oh," Lexie said and started smiling ear to ear.

"You guys go ahead," I said as I stood up from the booth. I walked towards them and unlocked the door, holding it open for them as they got their jackets.

"I can be back in five minutes if you need anything," Hugo said.

"I know. Thank you Hugo, but I'll be fine."

Hugo nodded has Lexie gave me a hug.

"Good luck," she whispered in my ear. "And you might want to lose the apron,"

"Crap," I said looking down at the mess that was my clothing after a long day. I untied the dirty apron and Lexie took it and quickly threw it in the dirty laundry bucket we had stashed under the front counter.

Jack got out of his truck when Hugo and Lexie started to leave. He gave them a small wave as he passed them on the way to where I was standing in the doorway waiting for him. Neither of us said anything. I stood back to let him in the diner then shut the door. I took a minute to relock it. My heart was racing. I took a deep breath in and let it out slowly to try to get it under control. It didn't work. I turned around to find Jack standing there watching me.

I leaned back against the door. He was clearly just coming off a long day working the farm. His jeans were dusty, work boots still on, and he was wearing the same coat he's worn to work the farm since high school. I was no better in my Crossroads Diner shirt and jeans covered in God knows what from dealing with food all day. My hair was falling out of the loose bun I put it in earlier in the day. We stared at each other for a minute, taking each other in.

"Would you like...", I started to say as I pushed myself off the door but I didn't get to finish.

Jack came up to me, cradling my face with his hands that were rough from years of farm labor, and kissed me. I think my brain shorted out for a second. It took me a minute to react. I could feel him about to pull away when I snapped out of it, wrapped my arms around his waist under his coat, and pulled him to me.

We pulled apart and Jack rested his forehead against mine and looked at me.

"I love you. I never stopped," he said quietly.

"It's always been you Jack," I said back.

We stood there holding each other. There was nothing else to say right now. We had our whole lives ahead of us. We would have our ups and downs but I knew, whatever life threw at us, we were now in it together.

"Come on," I said. "Let's get out of here."

He smiled at me and took my hand. We closed up the diner and left. The paperwork could wait until tomorrow.

# *Epilogue*

# SECRETS (BENNY)

*"The world is a dangerous place to live, not because of the people who are evil, but because of the people who don't do anything about it."*

— Albert Einstein

L exie and Hugo were leaving the diner as I stopped at a red stoplight. They passed Jack on his way inside.

"About time," I mumbled to myself as Tess let Jack inside the diner.

I watched Lexie get in her car. My heart felt like it skipped a beat like it always does when I see her. She was pushing me away, and I didn't know why. When she first came back, she avoided everyone which is something of an accomplishment in a town as small as Crossroads. Finally, about a month after she came back to town, I caved and went to her family's old house.

A long tree-line paved driveway led up to a grand house. Grand is not normally a word I use but it really was the only way to describe it. It looked like something out of Gone with the Wind with huge pillars gracing the front of a white two-story house with black shutters.

Despite the obvious neglect that came from sitting vacant for so long, the house was still impressive as it came into view.

Lexie opened the front door before I even made it up to the huge porch. She was wearing jeans and an overly large West Virginia University sweatshirt that completely engulfed her small frame. Her hair was pulled back into a messy ponytail.

She was the most beautiful woman in the world. The fact that I still felt that way kind of shocked me. I stopped halfway up the porch steps and Lexie stood in the doorway. We stared at each other, neither of us making a move or saying anything.

The she burst into tears, ran out the door in her bare feet, and wrapped her arms around my neck. The move was so unexpected, I didn't react for a minute. Finally, I put my arms around her waist and held her while she cried. Eventually, her tears slowed down and she pulled back and looked at me.

"I'm so sorry," she said so quietly I could barely hear her.

"What happened, Lexie?"

She looked down at her feet. "Do you want to come inside?" she asked.

I held my arm out in a lead the way gesture. She took my hand and we went inside.

That was months ago. Lexie had explained everything. All the things her dad was doing to make his money. The danger he put his family in. Where they went and what her life had been like for the years they were gone. None of it was good.

Ever since, we had seen each other all the time and talked every day. We had kept our relationship as friends, not going beyond that yet. She needed time. And she needed a friend. Especially in this town where the rumors were already swirling about her family's abrupt departure all those years ago and now her return alone.

Then she started working with Tess at the diner and things were getting better. Our relationship started to progress, and we were becoming a couple again though we were keeping it under the radar. We even shared a few hidden kisses when no one was looking.

A couple of weeks ago, all that changed. She started pushing me away. She couldn't talk when I called, stopped coming by the shop to bring me dinner, and avoided me when I came to the diner. Something was up. In my gut, I knew it couldn't be good.

The stoplight changed from red to green but I didn't start driving. I was still watching Lexie. She looked nervous. Maybe even scared. She was looking around the parking lot and seemed to rush to get into her car.

Did some of the trouble her father got in all those years ago find her? I didn't know but I was going to find out. Lexie did not need to handle whatever was going on alone. And I was not going to get up one day and find her gone again.

I grabbed my cell and called Lexie as I turned the Jeep around to head toward her house. Whatever secrets Lexie was keeping, whatever this trouble was, we would face it head on. Together.

*The second book in the Crossroads Series will be available in Fall 2024. Go to www.nightowlstories.com and sign up for my newsletter, The Hoot, to get the latest updates on book releases plus bonus stories about my favorite small town, Crossroads.*

# About the Author

T.S. Robinson is a lover of books of all kinds and genres but her heart belongs to romance. No matter the subject, every story can use a little romance. Her new book, *Something to Hope For*, is the start of a new series about a fictional small town in Virginia called, Crossroads. When she's not trying to steal time out of her day to write, she's one half of an all-star parenting duo that plays chauffeur, chef, and housekeeper for two daughters, two bearded dragons, and one Boston terrier.

You can connect with T.S. Robinson through her website, Night Owl Stories (https://www.nightowlstories.com/), or on Facebook (https://www.facebook.com/tsrobinsonnightowlstories) and Instagram (https://www.instagram.com/t.s.robinson/). She is always happy to connect and discuss books, writing, and the things that make life worth living.

*- T.S. Robinson*